Lizzy May Morrison lives in the West Country, with her dog and many friends nearby. She is now a grandmother and used to work in education. It may not come as a surprise (when you have read these pages) to learn that she drives an ancient car and flies an even older aeroplane.

For Eddie and Wilf; Kai and Lillie.
The next generation of readers.

Lizzy May Morrison

MY STORY

AUSTIN MACAULEY PUBLISHERS™

LONDON • CAMBRIDGE • NEW YORK • SHARJAH

A CIP catalogue record for this title is available from the British Library.

ISBN 9781398427563 (Paperback)
ISBN 9781398427587 (ePub e-book)

www.austinmacauley.com

First Published 2022
Austin Macauley Publishers Ltd®
1 Canada Square
Canary Wharf
London
E14 5AA

Grateful thanks:

To Tom for the illustration.

To flying friends, past and present, and their families.

Preface

She thought she could do it and that she had it in her—the stamina and endurance and self-belief—but now she is terrified. It's only in the last twenty minutes or so that she's had the courage to admit it; to herself that is: being the only person around.

How does it really feel, raw fear? The exhaustion, the befuddled concentration from hours of staring, her hunger and the cold—these are all aspects she might bring to mind later (if she lives). But right now, it's just the fear.

Fear of going forward because every mile brings her closer to that which is unrecognisable and riddled with risk. And yet she cannot turn back. She is beyond that, *The Point of No Return*. The other enemy would be waiting for her—the one which she has been fighting for over a year and from whom she is finally escaping.

Sometimes you have to do the wrong thing for it to be right.

She must press on, given what is below. What does death feel like when you have maybe five minutes, at most, to live? She doesn't want it to work out this way for no-one would find her, no one would know.

She has to keep going, she has to trust. If not in herself, then in the amalgamation of wood, cloth and metal that have kept her up thus far, and if not in the machine either, what else? Is there a greater power that can keep her safe?

And she recites the silly rhyme to herself that has become a sort of mantra going round inside her head. She mouths the words again—maybe they'll be her last.

Or could they help?

Lord of the sea and sky;
Help me fly.

Part One
Spring Term 1972

Chapter One
January

Hi there! My name is Lizzy and I am growing up in the 1970s. I guess it seems like an age ago. After all, that **is** in the last century. But when I put myself back into those days, life doesn't really appear to be so terribly ancient and old-fashioned.

At the time my story starts I am fifteen and a half. The Coal Miners are on strike at the moment which means that on some evenings we have power cuts.

I live at home with Mum and Dad and I go to college. I am the youngest there because everyone else is sixteen or over, but I have been given special permission to attend because my old boarding school was closing down. (It's not because I am super-clever or brainy). I don't have any brothers or sisters and I live out in the country in a small village which is OK as I have quite a few friends, including a special pal called Frankie—short for Francesca. Frankie is still at school (it's different from the one I went to).

I'm into the music of that time which, for me, is a combination of heavy rock such as Genesis, Deep Purple and Pink Floyd and the top songs in the charts from Slade, Rod Stewart and T. Rex. The fashion is baggy trousers, smock tops and skinny jumpers. Skirts are either really short minis or completely long and dragging on the ground. I also have a pair of platform shoes which are shiny and purple and would now be worth a fortune in a 'retro' shop. The fashion suits me because I am quite tall and very slim and can get away with skirts that only just cover my bum. In our house we have TV, but back then the word "computer" as we know it wasn't even in the dictionary. Frankie's parents have only just got a telephone and we are definitely not talking about mobiles!

I am studying for my 'O' levels at college and I guess I am about average for my age. Looking back, I don't think I worked extremely hard but I am probably giving myself less credit than I deserve. I was a very normal teenager and didn't find life particularly difficult; I had a good group of friends and I generally got on very well with my Mum and Dad.

Frankie has a boyfriend called Dave. Before she went out with Dave she was with Pete, and before Pete it was a guy called Alan. Frankie is only nine months older than me but she looks about seventeen, whereas I appear young for fifteen and the only benefit this brings is that I can still get on a bus for half price (child fare). Perhaps it's how I look or maybe it's just the way I am but I don't have a boyfriend. I'm happy having a good group of friends and lots of fun. I'm really keen on sport and sometimes it does seem that having a boyfriend can really be quite boring and antisocial. When Frankie and Dave are together, I feel like the odd one out and I wonder when I will get my best mate back.

So…boyfriends. The thing is, there's a guy in my Maths group called Joe and I really fancy him. He is different from the other boys I know. For one thing he's older. Joe is eighteen. That's three whole years my senior and, compared with me, he is **so** mature. But it's not just that. There's something about him that, to my mind, makes him seem extra special. I am intrigued by him too.

So far I have found out the following: a) he wants to be a teacher, b) in order to do this has to go to teacher training college, c) he doesn't have enough 'O' Levels/ 'A' Levels to get there and d) this is why he is in my Maths group (yippee for me). Joe is also good at Art. He's not just good at it, he is A1 brilliant and it is Art that Joe wants to be a teacher of eventually. There's no contest. Joe is cool, mature and talented and me—well I don't even look fifteen. There is no hope.

On the night of Wednesday, the 12th of January, I go to a party. It's a late Christmas 'do' for a sports group I belong to and good fun. We all want to dance even though the DJ keeps us waiting between each record change. (At these points we resemble versions of musical statues more than a disco). Frankie's Mum picks us up at 11:30 just as it's ending and I'm home by midnight and up for college at 7:30 the next morning.

Maybe it's the after-effects of the party, or perhaps just the way opportunities present themselves, but that following afternoon I find myself sitting next to Joe after our Thursday Maths lesson has ended and I'm talking to him properly for the first time. He seems interested in me! He asks lots of questions and I can tell he's paying attention when I gabble away with my stupid answers.

I want to keep talking—anything to stay sitting together. The one thing we establish is that I live in the same village where he goes to a youth club. I have never been to this particular club having been away at boarding school but it seems almost too good to be true. I can just 'turn up' on Friday evenings and 'happen' to see Joe. (He will never guess I've joined the club because of him, or will he? Do I care?) We keep talking and just being with him excites me. My exaggerated gestures must show how keen I am but he doesn't seem perturbed by my signals. In contrast to me he is calm, serious and grown up. How does a kid like me stand a chance, and why doesn't everyone in the whole world fancy Joe like I do?

When I go home that evening my heart is singing and my brain is leaping around with wild thoughts about Joe. Since the beginning of the course in September, I have watched him and never said very much. Now we have had a proper chat and, as far as I am concerned, I'm in love. I guess I'm just an ordinary teenager who is nuts about a boy; that's nothing unusual. But, for me this feels so special, so unique as if I am the only girl in the Universe who has ever had these feelings and fallen head over heels for a guy. This is **my** moment, my life and I can revel in the wondrous beauty of it all.

Unfortunately, things are not so good when I get home and I come down to earth with a bump. My Mum isn't well. She's been complaining of pains in her chest and I've got used to her not eating all her dinner and going to bed early because she is so tired. But today she's been back to the doctor to get the results of some tests. She doesn't tell me exactly what the problem is but I sense it's not good news.

All of a sudden I feel angry and cross with her. Why is she going to spoil things? Just when everything is about to go right for me my Mum has to go and get ill. This isn't fair. Dad comes into the kitchen and somehow, he seems different. He looks tired and old for my Father and it's all too much for me.

I'm tired from the party last night, the excitement of being with Joe, and I flip. I shout at my Mum. I can't believe I am doing this to her. My Mum who I love is so ill and tired and suddenly I'm screaming at her. So Dad shouts at me and it's awful. I'm hungry and thirsty but as far as they're concerned my day has ended and I'm off to my bedroom. I throw off my clothes and don't even bother to brush my teeth. As I slam the door however, I start to weaken and hot tears smart in my eyes. How **dare** my mother become ill and spoil everything just when my life is taking off? Why should I have to put up with pain and suffering when I could be out enjoying myself? Mum and Dad seem wrapped up in each other; who cares about me?

I lie straight and rigid under my sheet and blankets staring at the ceiling until the moon shines through my half-closed curtains casting shadows across the room. I turn over and put my face in my pillow and heave with sobs that seem to come out of my whole body. I am fifteen. It's January. I've spoken with a boy I've fancied for ages. And I now know deep in my heart that Mum is very sick indeed.

Chapter Two
Auntie Cath

I wake early. I'm thirsty and my stomach feels empty. It's Friday which I usually enjoy because I have good lessons on my timetable—English first of all which I enjoy. But I'm not really in the mood for college as I gather my thoughts in the darkness of a January morning and events of the previous evening cast a gloomy shadow over me. It's so early the heating hasn't come on, but I'm willing to brace the cold in order to have a hot drink. I put on my light, push my bedclothes away and get dressed. Just as I'm doing up the strap on my watch, I hear the rumble of our oil-fired boiler and I know it's 6:30 without even looking at my wrist.

I make myself a cup of coffee with lots of milk and two heaped spoonfuls of sugar which I gulp down while I put two slices of Hovis under the grill. Meanwhile, I feed our six-year old female cat called Tootsie.

Dad appears in the kitchen in his dressing gown. This is odd for a weekday as he works in an office, always wears a suit and is out of the house just after seven. But of course, owing to last night's events no one had a conversation with me and I am somewhat unaware of what exactly is going on. We sit down at the kitchen table and I give him one of my pieces of toast as a token peace offering. He explains that Mum has an appointment at the hospital and he is going with her. If he is back in time he will go to work in the afternoon. Meanwhile, she will stay in bed until they need to leave at 9:30.

It all seems rather strange and I don't feel like hanging around too much, so—most surprisingly for me—I am out of the house and up to the bus stop far earlier than normal. I resign myself to having a long and cold wait, but that is when Auntie Cath comes along.

* * * * * * * * * *

As well as all the obvious people you might expect to be in a fifteen-year-old's existence—family, friends, teachers, relatives and neighbours—there is another significant person in my life whom I haven't mentioned yet, and that is Auntie Cath. She isn't my real Aunt and we are not related in any way. Her full name is Catherine Van der Hayde. She lives in the same village as me and for two reasons we seem destined to be close.

The first occasion happened when I was nine years old. I had been sent on an errand by Mum to cycle up to the village shop and buy a box of icing sugar. On the way home a car came too close and I wobbled into it. I fell off and the car went over my bike but not over me. I was all right but rather bruised and very shaken. To make matters worse the car driver, a man, got out and started shouting at me.

Just at that moment along came Mrs Van der Hayde. I didn't know her then as she had only just moved into the village, but she stopped her car, saw that I was OK and then had such a fearsome 'go' at the driver I thought he was going to run from the spot leaving his car where it was! She picked up my bent bicycle and put it in the back of her Land Rover and then helped me climb in front whereupon she turned the car around and drove me home.

It was only a few weeks later (although by then I was ten years old) that the second big occasion happened between Mrs Van der Hayde and me, Miss Lizzy May Morrison. Quite simply I saved her life but it could have been anyone else; I just happened to be the person who was around at the time.

It was early September and for some reason that year the fields had some amazingly good mushrooms. I had persuaded my parents to let me put a bowl on our wall and I was selling them for 9d a bag. That was a long time ago, and yes, that **was** nine pence in old money! The mushroom business was going very well, in fact so well I had to keep roaming further and further to gather my crop.

On this particular day I went across a new field which brought me out at the end of a no-through lane with only one property. To get back onto the road I had to sneak through a rather overgrown garden, but as I crept around the corner of the cottage I fell over a ladder across the lawn and then—to my absolute horror—very nearly onto Mrs Van der Hayde herself, who was lying flat on her back. She was cold but conscious and had been there a long time. She was able to tell me she'd broken her leg and couldn't move.

I told her to lie still which was a very silly thing to say and ran as fast as I could to the first house at the top of the lane to get help. Within an hour she was in Hillerton Hospital and home a week later.

So a certain amount of destiny brought Mrs Van der Hayde and me together. In the following weeks my Mum, Frankie and I did a lot to help her. She invited Mum to call her Cath but Mum said I was too young to also call an adult by her Christian name only, so she became Auntie Cath. And she nearly always called me Lizzy May and my Mum Jennie, even when she was speaking about her to me.

* * * * * * * * * *

It's five years later but Auntie Cath still has the same old Land Rover, so on this notable morning I find myself hopping in to the cab and sharing the front seat with her three-year-old Poodle x Labrador called Spoodles.

"So Lizzy May, how are you and how is Jennie?" Auntie Cath is blunt and to the point and I always sense that she knows far more than she lets on, being very perceptive but in a non-judgemental sort of way. I know that some people have said they find her intimidating but maybe 'forthright' would be a more accurate description. And certainly I appreciated her straightforward attitude and down-to-earth approach and rarely found her scary.

So it all comes out; I'm relieved to be telling her about my Mum and the fact that hearing how ill she is really spoilt my day and that I had a row and now I feel awful. Auntie Cath doesn't say very much. She listens and focuses on driving in the town's traffic. She does a detour to drop me off at college. We get to the entrance and she switches off the engine. It is silent and she looks straight at me.

"You know Lizzy May," she says. "I don't care whether you think you've been a good person or a bad person. I'm more interested in who you are." And then she switches the engine back on and I say thank you and cheerio and get out.

I'm early at college on account of my lift and the caretaker—Isaac Chombele (pronounced 'Chombeely')—is only just unlocking the classrooms. Isaac is West African. He is always smiling and everyone likes him, but the rumour is that he lost everything at the start of the civil war in Nigeria and came to England only because he had a cousin who was able to give him a room and some support. I think that must have been about five years ago as I know that Isaac is now married and has a little girl.

"Hey Lizzy, how ya doing?" he asks and I find myself smiling back at him and telling him I'm OK. Isaac treats everyone as if they are special and he opens up the English room and turns the wall thermostat up so I can sit by the radiator and get warm. He whistles and jingles his bunch of keys and I wonder—how can someone who once lost all he had, start again and ever be happy?

He goes out and shuts the door to keep in the heat and I sit on my own in the classroom. I lean against the radiator and allow thoughts to wash around in my head. Auntie Cath's words repeat: "I don't care whether you think you've been a good person or a bad person. I'm more interested who you are." Is that really it? All my upset and anger at my Mum—does she love me for who I am and not for what I say and do? Perhaps that's the same with friends and when I come to think of it, that's how it is with Frankie. She and I are friends because we like each other as people. So maybe even though I flipped last night and said some horrible things to Mum it doesn't necessarily mean that I'm going to be rejected and unloved by those around me. It's me as a person that counts

22

and, much to my surprise, there seem to be lots of people who like me and want to know me better.

In the stillness of an empty English classroom and the heat of a radiator against my back, I start to feel happier, more comfortable and more **me**. Later on I'll go home and say sorry to Mum. I will offer to do something like wash up, and things will be fine and back to normal. It's the weekend so we'll all be at home. And then I also remember, it's the Friday evening Youth Club and I will see Joe…Whoopee!

Chapter Three
The Youth Club

The day dragged.

Having made up my mind I would make peace when I got home, I was anxious to be back as soon as possible and for everything to be normal. After lessons I chatted with a few friends whilst waiting for my bus, which turned up ten minutes late. I got out at the crossroads and walked down the lane in the January twilight. Five minutes later I was home but if I was expecting bright lights and a warm welcome, I was disappointed. The miner's strike was having its full impact and tonight it was our turn to suffer from the rationing.

We were having to make do with candles for light, the odd torch here and there and Dad had dug out the portable gas stove (normally kept with our tent) for cooking. Against the pale glow of the candlelight Mum's face looked even more tired and drawn than usual although I don't think mine was looking the picture of youthful brilliance either. Dad was in the kitchen and making a special effort to be cheerful. It felt a bit as if we were actors in a play waiting for the stage lights to come on and then we could speak out our lines we had been rehearsing all day.

But Scene One unfolded as the candle wax dripped onto improvised holders and we quietly ate our sausages cooked in a frying pan with heated up potatoes left over from the night before. We also had baked beans which are less appetising if served lukewarm. Dad had been shopping and bought Viennetta ice cream, chocolate and mint flavoured, something we normally only have on special occasions so he must have been trying to do something nice for me. Unfortunately, owing to the lack of electricity, all the food in the icing compartment of the fridge had started to defrost so the posh pudding was soft and melting by the time we came to our dessert and the happy moment that had been intended was somehow lost.

Mum asked me about my day and I know—I KNOW—I should have asked her about hers. But I didn't. I couldn't. I didn't want to know. I didn't want anything to spoil my anticipation for the evening ahead. So I spoke casually about some of my lessons and told them I'd had a lift with Auntie Cath. Then I asked if it was OK to go to the Youth Club that was happening later.

"That's the one near the Church, isn't it?" remarked Mum. "The one they hold in the Rectory Rooms—it's the old building near St Stephens that used to be the stables but has been converted into a sort of Church Village Hall."

Dad was dubious. He seemed to think it wouldn't be happening if there was a power cut and he was unhappy about me walking around the country lanes in the dark.

"I'll take a torch and I'll be fine," I insisted. But it was two against one and I knew that the only way I would be allowed to go out would be if Dad walked up when it finished and escorted me home. I felt like a child.

Just then the phone rang. It was Frankie who had heard from the 'bus-stop talk' that I was planning to go to the Youth Club and wanted to know if she could come too. I was delighted and said that I would call at her house on the way— it was in fact much closer to the Rectory Rooms than where we lived. If I thought, however, that this arrangement would sort out the embarrassment of having my father at my heels, I was mistaken.

"That's all right," he responded. "I don't mind you walking to Frankie's on your own as you can then go on together. But I'll still be there to get you and can walk you both back if Frankie's Mum agrees."

It was 6:30 p.m. and all my resolutions about offering to help wash up and be extra kind went out of the window. For one, we had very little light, and for another, the water wasn't hot enough. Yet another opportunity to do a job and comfortably chat away to Mum was missed.

I took a candle and went up to my bedroom to change. What to wear? How could I impress Joe? Somehow something deep inside me knew that actually whatever I might wear would not make a lot of difference (assuming I wasn't selecting something totally unsuitable) so I opted for the 'sensible reserve': Levi jeans, a pink 'skinny-rib' polo neck jumper and my Dr Martens boots. My hair was done up in a ponytail and I didn't bother with make-up. The light was so bad anyway I might have made a mess and I was guessing it might be pretty dim at the Youth Club too. I put on my thick anorak and picked up the torch with the brightest beam. I didn't have a handbag, just a purse in my pocket; no keys needed and certainly no mobile phone in those days.

At Frankie's house I was greeted with a surprise—the lights were back on! I blinked in the bright electric glare and knew that, whatever happened, the Youth Club would definitely be running. Frankie's Mum said, "You're early, why are you so keen Lizzy?" And I rather thought she sensed there was something up and not just a casual interest in the village Youth Club run by the Church. Frankie was on her own as Dave was having to stay at his home to babysit for his younger sister (I'd forgotten about Dave). Somehow Frankie's family seemed more laid-back and easy-going than mine. Maybe it was because there were more of them crowded into a much smaller house.

Even though the Youth Club had been running for two years and despite the fact that it was in the village where we had both lived for most of our lives, Frankie and I were surprised by how many young people there were who we didn't know. The reason became obvious; teenagers from nearby villages and the town were able to get a lift in a minibus driven and owned by the leader who was called Keith. I suppose altogether there were about twenty-five of us aged from fifteen (me) to sixteen, seventeen and eighteen (Joe). I spotted him in the far corner chatting to a couple of guys. When he saw me, he looked up and waved but he didn't come over.

Frankie and I went to 'The Bar' which sold tea, coffee and fizzy drinks, plastic cups of squash and a variety of sweets, chocolate and crisps. I bought two cups of squash and a packet of crisps to share with Frankie. There were two rooms, the one with 'The Bar' which had some easy chairs with low tables, and then another bigger room—The Games Room— consisting of two table tennis tables, a dart board and a table football. We chatted to each other and tried to pretend we were old hands and really used to being there. Everyone else seemed happily occupied playing games or sitting around in small groups. Then a couple of girls who went to Frankie's school came up and started talking and soon the four of us were laughing and joking and comparing funny stories of awful meals concocted by our parents when there was no electricity. Out of the corner of my eye I saw Joe had finished chatting to his friends and was coming across to us. I tried to seem casual but I could feel my heart beating a little faster.

"Hi, you came." He seemed pleased.

"Frankie," I said. "This is a friend of mine, Joe—he's actually in my Maths group at college."

When I said the word 'friend' I felt proud and part of the group and I could see that Frankie was quite impressed. We all talked together a bit more but I really wanted Joe to myself and suddenly I had an idea:

"Do you play table tennis?" I asked him.

"Sure, do you fancy a game?" He said it with a grin and I saw a less serious guy than I had encountered at college.

There was a free table and we each picked up a bat and began to play. Because my Mum was a Sport's Coach (before she became ill) I had been encouraged from a young age to play active games. I considered myself reasonable at table tennis mainly because I used to play after lessons at my old school. This evening, however, it was different and it took me a while to settle down. Joe was also quite good and he won the first game easily at 21 to 15. Then I got into my stride and was able to concentrate better so I won the next game beating him 21 to 16. (It was the old type of scoring system in those days).

"How about a decider, the best out of three?" Joe asked.

We changed ends again and this time the game got serious—we both wanted to win! We were 'neck and neck' with almost equal scores when there was an announcement for everyone to gather in The Bar for the evening's message. I suppose because Joe and I were playing table tennis it was natural for us to walk into the room together and fairly obviously to sit together. This was wonderful and I could hardly believe it. I felt people were looking at me—me the newcomer in the room sitting with Joe who seemed as if he belonged to the place and who, apart from the leaders, was probably the oldest in the room.

There was a short talk given by a visiting speaker. I had known that this youth club was run by the Church and I suppose I should have realised that at some point there would be a mention of God. I listened but it didn't make a huge amount of sense and anyway, here I was sitting next to a boy I madly fancied, so I certainly didn't need to dwell too much on religion at 8pm on a Friday evening in January. After the talk had ended a couple of guys and a girl stood up. The two chaps had guitars and the girl sang—nice folk sort of songs but I was impatient to finish the game of table tennis, beat Joe, and prove how good I was so that he would be most impressed!

Eventually we got back to the table and I beat him easily but my moment of glory was lost. The competitive element seemed to have gone from Joe and he became serious again.

"Well done," he said. "We must play again sometime." And with that, he wandered across the room to chat to another small group of lads and girls. I felt somewhat deflated, but wasn't going to display my disappointment so I went to find

Frankie who was sitting at a low table playing cards with another girl.

Just before 9pm everyone started packing up and putting things away in a store-room. I felt I should help so I went to the bar and asked the lady if there was anything I could do. It turned out that she was the wife of the leader/mini bus driver. She appeared very friendly and asked if I could rinse out the plastic cups as they all got re-used. I was happy to help and we worked together with me washing up and her packing, sorting and counting the money. We chatted comfortably and I found out that her name was Amanda. She asked me if I would be coming again and when I replied, "Definitely," she seemed pleased. (I didn't tell her why).

It was time to go and I looked around for Joe hoping I would get a special and personal good-bye from him. But he was with another guy getting equipment into the cupboard and all I got was a quick wave, and saw his lips mouth the word "Bye," and then he was lifting another table to put away and concentrating on that. Once again, I didn't want to make it appear that I was needy or expecting anything so I casually got my coat and asked Frankie if she was ready.

It was a little after 9 and Dad was waiting outside moving from one foot to another to keep warm. I wondered if he had been there for a while.

"Hi girls," he said. "Had a good time?"

"Yes, thank you, Mr Morrison," replied Frankie in a rather over-polite voice—ever the Charmer. (She would never have called him Chris).

It was five minutes to walk to her house and we didn't bother to go up her path. She said goodbye to us and we walked on down the lane by torchlight and in silence. I was thinking about the evening and the mixture of the highs and not-so-highs of being with Joe.

Just before the entrance to our house Dad stopped. He seemed to be struggling to say something.

"Lizzy," he said in a very solemn voice. "It's not good news about Mum. I know you've been avoiding this but you have to know. The Doctors have given us six months."

Chapter Four

Tears

Snuggled under my sheet and blankets I was having a lovely dream. I must have been at some sort of summer camp and I was with a bunch of friends. We were in a big field playing games, maybe football, laughing and having fun. Joe was there, I know he was, and then Amanda was calling us to come and have food. The calling got louder and I heard my name but this time it was Dad telling me to come and have breakfast. The cosy warmth subsided as I remembered his last words to me and the realities of my life in January 1972 came back to me. What on earth made me dream about camping in summer? Surely the presence of our gas stove last night wasn't enough to trigger that thought!

I put on my dressing gown and went downstairs. Once again, it was only me and my father in the kitchen.

"Toast?" he asked me. "One slice or two?"

"I'm thinking of going to see Frankie this morning," I said. "Is that OK?"

"Of course," replied Dad. But I could see he was thinking: *when* is she going to talk with her mother?

I slipped out without properly saying goodbye having put on my wellies, warm gloves and coat. It was a grey day, cold and not bright as it can sometimes be in the winter. Once out in the lane, however, I actually wasn't sure I wanted to see Frankie. For one thing there was little privacy in her house and secondly, I was uncertain what I would say or how I would say it. So instead of walking up the road I crossed over into the field and cut across the 'mushroom way' to Auntie Cath. Of course she wouldn't be expecting me but I could always offer to take Spoodles for a walk if she was busy. Auntie Cath seemed to have some sort of journalism job that occupied a lot of her time and if she wasn't outside doing jobs to her old cottage and garden she would be absorbed by her desk with a typewriter on the table and masses of papers all over the place.

As it happened, she wasn't outside or in her office/sitting room but brewing up a pot of strong coffee on her old-fashioned stove in the tiny kitchen of her ancient home. She looked up when she saw me about to knock and opened the door with a smile (Auntie Cath never locks her house), and not at all surprised to see me.

"Just in time for a coffee, well done! Put your muddy boots on that newspaper and draw up a seat by the fire."

I did exactly that and a huge wash of relief came over me as I knew here was someone I could talk to.

"I don't know the details," I said straight away before she could enquire. "But Dad told me last night the doctors have given Mum six months."

Auntie Cath looked very serious. She stood by the stove, coffee jug in hand but in no hurry to pour or do anything.

"I knew it was bad," she replied. "We had a meeting last week for the Summer Fete and your mother sent her apologies stating that she would not be able to help at all this year. I thought to myself, for Jennie Morrison to cry off like this and not even send in any plans, she must be seriously unwell. And then when I saw you yesterday, although you weren't able to give me any information, you'd be surprised how much you can reveal even when you don't know all the facts."

She was right. Despite not yet having *that conversation* with Mum I knew deep down she was terribly unwell. Mum and I were close and we would often find we were thinking the same things even if we weren't talking about them. Perhaps I had been carrying my worries for longer—and deeper—than I thought, and maybe I'd let them show more than I had intended.

Auntie Cath poured the coffee and put two sugars into mine without needing to check. I put my feet on the rung of the stool and sat with the mug on my knees and my hands wrapped around it. The smell of roast coffee mingled with the homely scent of the wood, burning in her stove. Suddenly I felt able to let go. The tears fell down my face and dripped into my lap. Auntie Cath, now seated, sat still opposite me. We said nothing and no-one moved. It was a peaceful moment, quiet, except for the clock ticking on the wall and Spoodles giving the occasional contented sigh or shuffle as he lay in front of the hot fire. Finally, Auntie Cath broke the silence:

"When you get home you must talk to Jennie."

We sat and drank our coffee. The warm kitchen, the presence of a friend and a dog on the floor calmed me down. The tears stopped flowing and I sniffed at my very runny nose wiping it all across my sleeve. Perhaps even that was too much for a practical lady in her 50s and she suddenly became more business-like.

"I don't have any tissues in the kitchen," she said. "But there are some in the bathroom. Go upstairs and help yourself; second door on the right along the corridor."

I tramped up the rickety wooden staircase which led directly from her living room (there being no hall-way). I'd never been beyond the kitchen and the adjoining sitting room before. The cottage was small and old and rather in need of some repair in places. Upstairs the first room was clearly her bedroom. The door was open and there was a large iron bedstead where various knitted blankets of assorted colours lay unmade on the bed. Opposite the bathroom was another door slightly ajar, that's because the frame looked so wonky the door couldn't shut properly. I guessed that was a spare room as I knew it was only a two-bedroom dwelling.

I got the tissue and blew my nose and felt more comfortable. Then something came over me which I couldn't resist. It wasn't actually nosiness, maybe more a sense of idle curiosity and that unexpected moment of opportunity. I pushed open the door a little more and glanced into the unoccupied room. It was as one might expect of a spare room; a bed with two or three folded blankets, a huge wardrobe (how did anyone get that up the stairs?) and a chest of drawers.

Various cardboard boxes were against the wall under the window and there was an old rug on the floor with uneven fringes at either end as if a dog had chewed away at the tassels. But then something else caught my eye; a picture on the wall, so interesting that I went closer into the room to stand in front and get a better look. It was, in fact, a black and white photograph (although I would say more like a faded brown and cream in colour) and it was hanging at the same level as my head in a wooden frame about the size of a piece of A4 file paper.

The photo showed a young woman standing next to an old looking aeroplane with four wings and an open cockpit. The woman was wearing trousers and a leather flying jacket. She was standing tall and straight and appeared to be looking resignedly at the camera as if she had been asked to pose but didn't want her photograph taken. Despite the flying helmet hiding her hair, I knew who it was. In her right hand she held a map and in her left was a small bag of some description. Without a doubt, that young lady in the picture was about to get in and fly the aircraft.

I looked closer and noticed a small inscription on the frame: **Haarlem 1939**. *Goodness,* I thought, *who is this person whose past I know nothing about?* But then I realised I was snooping and it was none of my business. Anyway, I had more important things to occupy my mind so I went downstairs and put my coat and boots back on as it looked like my host wanted to get on and 'Do' things. I decided to walk along the lanes, it would take a bit longer and that would give me more time to think. As I walked home, I thought a lot about what I would say when I got back.

Dad was still in the kitchen but it was clear that a lot of activity had taken place while I had been out. Packets from the larder were in disarray on the table and my father was concentrating on measuring ingredients into a mixing bowl. He looked as if he was conducting some sort of scientific experiment, only he wasn't using test tubes but a very large pudding basin.

"Mum thought I should make a quiche," he muttered. "She said it works well because you can eat it hot or cold."

At this point he looked up. In his exasperation he'd wiped his hair from his face with a floury hand so there were streaks of white powder across his forehead. He had also selected one of Mum's aprons—potentially sensible except it was bright pink with white roses and a frilly bit around the neckline. I stood and looked at my poor father who had probably never made pastry in his life and I couldn't help it; the scene was disturbingly funny and I tried, very unsuccessfully, to control my sniggers. He seemed so helpless; my meticulous father who worked in an office and would ask one 'of the girls' to make coffee for his clients (that's how it was in those days).

"Let me help," I suggested. "We can do it together."

But the first thing I had decided to do would be to take a hot drink to Mum. It was important to me that I did it without finding some other reason to stall the operation so I put on the kettle (no power cut) and made a cup of tea. Dad shook his head when I gestured an extra cup to him.

"I won't be long," I said.

Mum was sitting up in bed. A book lay open beside her but there were other papers—typed-up sheets that looked formal—on her lap.

"Oh Lizzy, thank you!" she exclaimed when I entered the room. "I've been so wanting a drink but I felt I couldn't bother your father."

I put the cup and saucer on the bedside table and without even thinking, knew what I would do. I kicked off my slippers and got into bed with her. We pulled the blankets up and lay hugging each other.

"It's not in my chest," she said. "It's lower down and they say they can't do anything. My poor, poor Lizzy."

And so, for the second time that morning tears trickled down my face but this time they mingled with those from my Mum. We didn't need to say anything, we held each other tightly and, once again, it was the things we didn't say which were more important. Gradually the crying eased, we both calmed down and she sat up to drink her tea. But I found the comfort of the warm bed too much to resist and, with my head on the pillow, dozed off. A weight had been lifted from me.

The conversation I had been dreading had happened but not in some cold medical way that I had anticipated. And instead of me feeling sorry for my Mum, it was her feeling sorry for me. She understood my fears, my reluctance to talk about her illness and my trepidation about knowing the facts. In time, I knew I would be able to understand and learn more, meanwhile I had to accept the fact that she loved me and that she was extremely unwell.

It was an hour later that I remembered my promise, my father struggling with his culinary efforts. I hastily got out of bed and put on my slippers and went downstairs.

"I'm sorry…" I started to say and looked around. No one was there. The kitchen was tidy again and the washing-up had been done. And there, on the table was a perfectly cooked quiche which looked delicious.

Dad had done it all on his own without my help. Of course he had.

Chapter Five

Elsa Duke

After my somewhat emotional weekend, I was rather looking forward to the normality of college but if I thought it was going to be a nice and ordinary Monday for me I was mistaken.

I haven't yet told you about Elsa Duke.

I suppose I have always assumed that most of us go through school making various friends along the way. We may lose some friends and gain new ones and generally there are a few close ones—ones who may stay with us for life. So it came as a bit of a surprise that not long after I had started college, I appeared to have an enemy. To me it was quite bewildering because I knew I'd never done anything to upset Elsa Duke. For one thing I hardly knew her and for another we hadn't even been to the same school together, but I felt she hated me a very particular way. I really couldn't work it out.

As it happened, Elsa had been to school with Frankie although of course Elsa was a year older. I asked Frankie about her one day, trying to sound very casual about it. But Frankie couldn't shed any light either and just muttered something about Elsa being very brainy and having a different set of friends to her—nothing unusual there.

Elsa and I had little in common. She was in fact nearly two years older than me. My birthday is in June and hers in September so consequently I was always one of the youngest in my year group and she would have been one of the eldest. Added to that, I was a year younger than everyone anyway at college owing to my special circumstances, so I was only a little over fifteen when I first attended and Elsa was just seventeen. But it wasn't the age difference that made her so despise me, I was sure. We were different in other ways too.

Elsa was more mature looking and wore glasses. Her hair was short and she had a very studious look about her. She wasn't skinny like me which helped to make her look even older. Teachers seemed to warm to her and she was often picked to represent the class for various events, so for example if we had a visiting speaker to one of our lessons it would be Elsa who would be asked to propose a vote of thanks. But still, despite our differences, I could not work out why Elsa Duke was specifically unpleasant to me when she seemed to be perfectly reasonable with everyone else.

One day things got so bad I pushed Frankie a bit more when we met up at the weekend.

"Elsa Duke really seems to hate me," I told Frankie, "and I can't for the life of me work out why."

Frankie considered.

"Maybe she's just jealous," she replied.

I was astounded. "Why on earth should she be jealous of me? She hardly knows me."

"Maybe not you, but she knows your Mum."

Things still seemed unclear. Lots of students knew my Mum because she was a freelance netball and tennis coach and visited lots of schools, that is until recently before she became ill. Originally, she trained as a PE teacher but when I was about two she suffered with bad headaches so she stopped working full-time (she had me to look after anyway). As I grew older and went to primary school she started part-time work going around the county giving advice to teachers and doing the coaching. I pressed Frankie again.

"I still can't see why knowing my Mum makes her so angry to me," I replied.

Frankie looked at me.

"Oh sorry, I thought you knew. Elsa's Mum is in a wheelchair. She's paralysed from the waist down."

So there I had it; a girl who was incredibly jealous and hated me for having a sporty and fit Mum, or so she thought. I vowed that she would not find out about my Mum's illness. Thankfully, the subjects I was studying at college were 'O' levels unlike Elsa who was doing mainly 'A' levels so the chances of seeing each other because we had no choice were limited only to our History lessons…

Every Monday morning we had double History. It was a big class and a popular subject, mainly down to the fact that we had a wonderful teacher called Mr Cook. Not only was he reasonably young (for a teacher) he was also a quite brilliant historian and very gifted lecturer. Since secondary school I had always loved History and been lucky with my teachers. It was not unusual for me to do extra research for my homework and I could often be found in the library reading around a subject so that I had additional material for my assignments.

Mr Cook had noticed me doing this. He was also researching for his doctorate (how brainy) and his specialism was European Social History of the Second World War. There had been a piece about him recently in our local newspaper where he'd asked people to contact him if they knew of a war story of escape or heroism in the late 1930s and early 1940s. I supposed that once Mr Cook got his PhD we would have to call him Dr Cook and that all seemed rather spectacular.

Not only was Mr Cook an inspirational teacher because of his vast knowledge, he was also quite innovative in the way he delivered his lessons often getting us to do role plays or mock interviews with famous people from history. I really liked his teaching style. So, it was no surprise that on this particular Monday morning, he strode into the classroom and announced:

"Right Chaps and Chapesses, let's get on with our presentations."

I was sitting next to a friend Carol, and together we'd done some extra research on the Monmouth Rebellion as this was the era we were studying for our 'O' level syllabus, but Mr Cook, always eager to keep us on our toes, sprang an extra surprise.

"I'm going to split you all up today and get you working with a different partner. Carol, you come over here and sit with Kevin."

He went on round the classroom mixing us all up and taking no notice of any personal preferences we may have had. Mr Cook came to Elsa Duke:

"Oh look, there's a spare seat next to Lizzy. Elsa, take your stuff and go and sit next to her."

If people in my class hadn't known before of Elsa's pure animosity towards me they would have known now. Mr Cook had too much authority and charisma for any of his students to argue with him but her body language said far more than words. She absolutely glared at her teacher and for a few moments I wondered what she was going to do. Then she stood up rigid and with an *enormous* sigh picked up her papers, kicked her chair back and stomped across the classroom. She slammed her books on the table next to me and made a huge and deliberate manoeuvre with her chair so that she could be positioned at the extreme edge of the table. Mr Cook chose to ignore this and carried on assigning the random couples.

The next thirty minutes was the only occasion up till then that I never wanted to be in a History lesson, any History lesson. It was unbearable. To say that Elsa was uncooperative was an understatement and I was embarrassed. Carol and I had done a lot of preparation for this assignment and I was determined not to let it go to waste. When it was our turn to stand up and give our bit of the presentation, I took control. I became the interviewer and interviewee feeding the answers to the questions I posed to Elsa and hardly giving her the chance to give her own opinion. When it came to the end I announced,

"Well, thank you Elsa, for taking the time to be interviewed. Is there anything further you would like to add?"

And she simply said *no*, gathered up her things and went back to wait by her old seat before anyone could stop her. Mr Cook said thank you and moved on to the next pair.

As the lesson was ending and we were all packing up, Mr Cook said, "Lizzy Morrison, would you mind staying back? I'd like to have a word with you."

Oh dear, I thought, *now I'm in for it. He's going to say I was overbearing and dominant and wouldn't let Elsa get a word in edgeways*, but I was surprised to see a more sensitive side to my teacher than I would previously have given him credit.

"That was a jolly good effort you gave Lizzy. I'm sorry I put you with Elsa, but quite frankly you are two of the strongest students in the group and I thought you would work well together. What went wrong?"

"I honestly don't know Sir," I replied and suddenly my theory about Elsa being jealous of me seemed rather thin and I certainly wasn't going to disclose private opinions on our mothers to my History teacher.

"Well, I don't know either. Perhaps she's just having a bad day," he commented and left it at that. Mr Cook was too professional to single out a student for discussion and I wasn't in the mood to dwell on the subject.

But as he was collecting his papers he said:

"By the way I've noticed you doing extra research in the library for our topics. Well done Lizzy, I like your methods. You'd make a good historian. Stick with it." And with that he snapped shut his briefcase and went out of the classroom.

Chapter Six

February

After the History lesson incident Elsa Duke seemed to leave me alone for a while. Maybe she had overdosed on her anger towards me or perhaps she might have felt she overstepped the mark with her display and it hadn't done her any favours. Whatever the reason, it was nice to have a bit of peace for a few weeks.

That sense of calm was what I needed in my life more than anything. We seemed to be on a bit of a roller-coaster with Mum's illness. Some days she was terribly unwell and in pain; other days she was much better with more energy and she would potter around in the kitchen or be at her desk writing letters. Every afternoon when I got back from college we would sit down together on the sofa and I would tell her about my day (not the Elsa situation though), what I was doing and the different homework projects I was working on. She was very interested in everything and one evening I found myself telling her about Joe.

Of course there wasn't much to tell her. It would have been nice to report that there was a budding romance in the air but nothing could be further from reality. It's true we saw each other in Maths lessons and also that we met socially every Friday at the Youth Club. But those evenings generally followed a very similar pattern. He would arrive first, being reliant on a lift in the minibus which had to get there early for unlocking and setting up. Then, I would turn up and spot him and say *Hi* as casually as I could.

At some point in the evening we would detach ourselves from the groups of friends we were with and play table tennis. Sometimes he would win and sometimes I would, and sometimes the contest would be so close we would lay down our bats and call it a draw. There would then be the churchy bit in The Bar followed by a bit more chatting with friends and finally, packing up. I couldn't see how anything was going to develop beyond this rather inflexible structure we had created. But I was determined not to appear to be a pushy person and Joe seemed to be quite happy with the way things were.

"Do you think he has a girlfriend in his hometown?" Mum asked one evening after we'd snuggled down on the sofa in front of the fire with a hot drink and a blanket across us both.

"No," I said emphatically. It's certainly not something I hadn't considered but I was quite sure there was no one else. For one thing, Joe would have invited her to the Youth Club and for another, well I was just *sure*. It was a feeling.

Mum was very encouraging and wise.

"Oh Lizzy, I'm sure if it's meant to happen it will. The best relationships always take time to develop. I was sixteen when I met your dad and it was two whole years before he asked me out on a date, fancy that! Mind you, he's always been very careful about things and likes to have considered all the options before making a decision. But once he's done that, I think he's confident he's made the right one."

She sat lost in thought staring at the flames of our open fire. I didn't want to say anything to spoil the moment, both of us aware that life as we knew it wasn't going to stay the same, but at the same time realising how special their marriage had been.

I knew how close Mum and Dad were to each other and that they'd fallen in love while still teenagers and kept their relationship going through the challenge of universities and tough careers.

"My Lizzy," said Mum. "You **will** find the perfect one, and be happy. I know it in my heart."

Of course the tears fell again with the intimacy of the moment but they were gentle, nothing to be extinguished in a hurry. Just the two of us, sitting together on the sofa sharing a blanket, musing about life and recognising how different our futures would be.

"Actually there's something to tell you," said Mum thoughtfully after a while. "I haven't said anything up to now as I hadn't wanted to get your hopes up, but I had an appointment last week and Mr Hargreaves, my consultant, wants to try me on a new drug. It won't cure me, but it might prolong my ability to fight this disease, and it also should help to lessen the pain. He said he wanted me to think about it because, as always with drugs—especially new ones—there may be side effects and I could have an adverse reaction. But I've thought about it and really I've got nothing to lose. What do you think?"

"Oh Mum, that would be great!" I replied and then I added "But you must do what you think is best for you."

"I will," she responded. "Oh, my darling Lizzy, you really are being so brave and mature. I love you so much. I worry about you too. I feel I'm putting too much on your shoulders. Everyone is helping me and Dad is being so wonderfully strong through all this too. I do hope there's someone you can turn to and lean on."

As a matter of fact, I had been mulling over the same concern. It's true the three of us had become extremely close. Not only that, but we were being honest too and especially kind to each other. If there hadn't been that awful scenario of the Big Disease hanging over us, I think we would have been the happiest family on earth. Nevertheless, I didn't have an outlet. Of course I had Frankie who by now was always asking about my Mum but despite her being my best mate I felt she couldn't identify with how I was feeling. After all, how could she know what I was going through when she had nothing to compare it with for herself? Added to that she seemed to be going through a particularly intense period with Dave and I hardly ever saw them apart.

There was Auntie Cath too, but she also seemed to be engrossed in a Very Important Project and I'd already had a good cry in her kitchen. I suppose I wanted to find someone who had had a similar experience. I needed to know how they'd been able to cope and what had helped and above all what actually happened if that dreadful moment of death came before you were ready (could you ever be ready?) Was it terrifying? What would it be like for Mum, for Dad, for me?

I didn't say any of this to Mum, it wasn't really the right conversation even though we were becoming much closer and anyway at that moment Dad came in from work. But funnily enough in the place where logically perhaps, I should have been most expecting it, I found a listening ear. It was a Friday night at Youth Club. By now January had turned into late

February and I was getting to know more people having attended for about six weeks and really starting to feel like a Regular. I often helped wash up at the end, it being the sort of environment where everyone mucked in and did their bit. Two nights after my sofa talk with Mum I was at the club and helping Amanda to do the usual packing up routine.

"Thanks so much for helping, Lizzy," Amanda said after I had cleared up a lot of empty packets and carried the bin outside. "I'm so exhausted at the moment; all I want to do is put my head down and sleep!"

I looked at her in surprise and then I guessed: "You're …expecting a baby?" I asked tentatively (how embarrassing if I was wrong).

"Yes. Can't you tell!" she exclaimed. "It's our first. Everyone is thrilled. Although," she added with a tinge of sadness, "Mum won't be around to see it. She died last year and I still really miss her."

Chapter Seven
The Intruder

It would be another week before I could be with Amanda in a quiet corner but I was happy to wait, and I also felt that I could now go and see Auntie Cath without fearing I would sob away by her kitchen stove again. I could give her a bit of an update on Mum even though I was a little hazy of the latest developments. So the following afternoon, Saturday, I trudged across the fields to her little old cottage.

Spoodles barked and barked as I approached and seemed very unsettled—but if I thought the dog was a little out of character that was nothing compared with the behaviour of Auntie Cath.

"Who's that?" she demanded in a fierce voice. "Oh Lizzy it's you. Come in, come in. Good to see you." She looked calmer at my presence. I walked into her cottage and into a scene of utter upheaval.

Auntie Cath's home was never the tidiest I'd come across but it was normally in a state of well organised clutter. She always knew where everything was and liked to have her papers close to hand when she was writing, so there were nearly always piles of books, magazines and other important looking documents littering her desk and various other surfaces of her sitting room. But today it was a different picture. It was as if someone had gone in with a huge industrial blow-dryer and pumped everything into the air and not cared where it landed. I stood and looked at the scene and gasped.

"Yes," said my friend grimly. "I suppose I should have been more vigilant but I never expected it after all these years …" She tailed off picking up random bits of paper and looking a little confused as to where to place them next.

"You've been burgled," I stated.

"Yes, you could say that," she replied a little irritated. "But to be more precise whilst I was out, I had an intruder. Nothing's been stolen, at least nothing of any significance. He didn't find what he was looking for because mercifully he wasn't looking in the right place," she added, a little more quietly and thoughtfully.

I was utterly perplexed.

"Let me help you clear up," I suggested, and thankfully she agreed, getting me to do the more easy and obvious tasks such as gathering the magazines and putting them into order while she sorted the papers and filed them into her own particular system (that is 'filing' as in small bundles with rubber bands, not in filing cabinets with alphabetical order as my father's office).

The task didn't take as long as I thought and after an hour Auntie Cath stood up stiffly having been kneeling for too long inside a circle of paper. She stretched and sighed.

"I think we're nearly there Lizzy. Thank you for your help. Let's put the kettle on and sit in the kitchen."

I was quite glad to be out of the sitting room, there was an odd smell in there which I couldn't place.

We took up our normal seats by the stove with Spoodles, much calmer now, at our feet. Auntie Cath was visibly relaxed too, happier even, and as we sipped our tea started to enquire about Mum and I was able to give her some tentative good news. We chatted about a few other things as well but if I thought my friend was going to tell me anything about her morning's Intruder I was wrong. As far as I could tell, it was a closed conversation and I knew better than to pry, but as I was leaving, I did say two things which got different reactions.

"Are you going to tell the police about this, Auntie Cath?" I inquired as I was putting on my coat.

"Police!" she exclaimed as if I was instead referring to aliens. "Good heavens no—they wouldn't be in the least interested."

And then, as I put on my wellington boots, I said, "Well, I think you should start locking your house from now on Auntie Cath." She looked at me intently and then, with a softening expression said, "Yes, Lizzy. Yes, you are right. I will from now on whenever I go out. That is a good plan. Thank you for your help, always good to see you. Love to Jennie."

She shut her door and I was left to walk home. I took the lanes so I had further to walk and more time to think.

Without doubt Auntie Cath was an unusual person. Why would she have an Intruder? What was there to steal? I didn't know her personal circumstances but I was fairly sure she didn't have bags of cash lying around. If she had money, she would have spent it on some home improvements. As for valuable antiques or jewellery, again I couldn't see the connection. It seemed as if she knew who the Intruder was and it also occurred to me that he was most likely searching for an important piece of paper.

Chapter Eight

Messages

The next week was a good one as far as college was concerned. First of all, I received a piece of History homework from Mr Cook and I had the highest marks in the class. Actually, being top of the form was not my particular ambition; it was the comment that he wrote at the bottom which pleased me more:

'This is a particularly impressive piece of work. The depth and detail of your presentation demonstrates insight and interest. You have gone above and beyond with your research and this has enabled you to produce an account of exceptional quality. This standard is comfortably equivalent to A-level and I thoroughly recommend that you continue to study this subject next year. Well Done Lizzy.'

I had a lot of respect for Mr Cook and knew that he meant what he said or wrote, so I was especially pleased. I didn't show these remarks to anyone else, but I thought I would tell Mum when I got home. Dad, too—maybe I was becoming a bit like him in my considered approach to work.

The second event which gave me something nice to think about was an interesting art project set by Mrs Paynter. (Yes, it's true that was her name but it sounds funnier when spoken than it looks in written form). Mrs Paynter, our Art Teacher, gave us an assignment entitled 'Developments in Fashion through the Last Hundred Years'. As well as this being relevant to the syllabus we were studying, she said that our sketches and final work would be put up on a display for the forthcoming Parents Evening at the start of the summer term. She went around the class giving us each a particular decade to explore. When it was my turn, she gave me the 1950s and as I was born in 1956, I thought it could be quite interesting. I could use old family photos and do lots of research because there would be plenty of material available which I could use.

"Now I don't just want a lot of pictures cut out of magazines," she continued. "You need to present sketches and accompanying notes and if possible, show some development. This is an Art Project. Ten years is a long time and people's tastes and habits can change a lot in a decade. Please produce one large final poster which brings together all your investigations."

During my lunch break I went into the college library to see what I could find, but after searching for a while I became a bit disappointed by the lack of material available on the shelves and decided I would need to pay a visit to the town library when I got the chance. Just as I was about to leave, in walked Joe.

"Hi," I said.

"Hi," he replied and we both looked a little embarrassed. "Doing anything interesting?"

So I told him about the project and because Joe was doing 'A' Level and clearly passionate about anything to do with art, he showed a keen interest. I told him I had to produce one final picture along with my notes and sketches.

"Hmm," he said thoughtfully. "I suppose you could do a collage so that it looks something like a storyboard with all the aspects coming together in one big poster. You could even have different headings in a variety of writing styles and colours showing how fashion has developed through the years."

"That's a brilliant idea!" I said, "My painting isn't all that good but I like design and I reckon I could do something interesting with lots of material on one large display." And I told him about my plans to use the town library.

"I could help you if you like," he said. "We could go and do some research together."

There was a stifled cough behind me and I turned to see Elsa Duke with her face apparently absorbed in a book she had selected from the shelf. I didn't think she wanted me to notice her standing so close, but I picked up my things and said goodbye to Joe and walked down the corridor humming a tune with a broad smile on my face. Would I like Joe's help? Yes I would, and nothing was going to come between Joe and me—not even Elsa Duke. Or so I thought.

* * * * * * * * * *

The 'Town Library Research Opportunity' didn't materialise that week owing to other things going on and it was Friday before I knew it. Obviously, I saw Joe in the Maths lessons but we always behaved like model students without giving anyone a hint that there was anything between us. Well, there wasn't, was there? Or maybe…?

That night I walked up to the Youth Club on my own. Dad was still insisting on walking back in the dark with me but I knew when the clocks went forward and the evenings got lighter he would be less worried and might relent, letting me walk home on my own. Not that I minded so much these days. It was quite nice to have Dad to myself and we would often walk back together in companionable silence.

Frankie had been giving the Youth Club a miss for a few weeks and I wondered what was going on. We seemed to be less close than we had been and I was thinking about the influence her relationship with Dave was having on our friendship.

But it was Amanda who I wanted to talk to and for that reason I was prepared even to forego the table tennis sessions with Joe. When I arrived, I went straight up to The Bar. "Hello," she said, pleased to see me as always.

"Amanda," I hesitated. "Could I have a word with you in private? There's something I want to talk about."

"Of course," she replied. "I'll get someone to mind the counter and we can go and sit in that quiet corner over there. Look, I'll just make a couple of hot drinks for us."

Just at that moment Joe came into the room and she asked him to help at the bar (which of course he was only too willing to do).

So Amanda and I sat down and sipped hot chocolate (she said she was 'off coffee' at the moment) and I told her all about my Mum and her illness, her visits to the doctor, the stuff I knew and the stuff I didn't. I poured it all out earnestly and she listened intently without needing to ask any questions or double-check she was getting the facts right.

Now and then Joe would glance across at us in a concerned manner.

"So you see," I concluded. "I've been so worried. There's really been no one who I thought would understand and I've kept quiet about it at college because I don't want a fuss and anyway that is the one place where I can forget about my worries about Mum and live a normal life."

"Oh Lizzy," Amanda responded. "I know what you've been going through. I thought the same even though I'm older than you and married to Keith. I still felt so worried about my Mum, but you know it's really important not to be left in the dark. Don't let your parents protect you by keeping the worst from you. It sounds like you have a great relationship with them but you don't always have to be positive. Although it's hard to get the bad news it's easier to come to terms with if you are living with it daily or weekly. My faith helped me a lot. When Mum died, I felt like someone was watching over me and helping me through the bad times."

We talked some more. I didn't really get the religious bit but I did feel immensely comforted and a huge sense of relief seemed to settle on me. Before we finished, Amanda asked if I would mind if she shared our discussions with Keith and one or two others.

I didn't really mind and I trusted her judgement that she would be discreet but I wasn't sure that telling others would do much good.

On the way home I talked more confidently and maturely to Dad than I ever had before. I asked specific questions about

Mum's prognosis, her treatment, the new drug she was having and how much hope there was. After all, time was marching on, we were now in March and June was only three months away. For my father, ever the calculating realist, he was cautiously optimistic.

"We don't know Lizzy, but we have another appointment with Hargreaves next Wednesday. It seems some blood tests they have done have shown signs of improvement. It's still early days and we will know more in a few days. We just have to hope."

Chapter Nine
The Shock

The weekend progressed and before I knew it, we were half way through another week of college. Wednesday afternoons were always designated as 'timetable free' for other activities. This meant that sporting fixtures could be arranged and any other extra-curricular pursuits followed. Because I was quite sporty, I generally found Wednesday afternoons one of the busiest times of the week. On this particular day we were due to play a home netball match against a school from another town. I was already changed into my netball kit and we were waiting in the lobby at 1.45 when Miss Russell, our games teacher, came in.

"I'm really sorry girls," she announced. "But I've just had St Cuthbert's on the phone. Apparently there's something wrong with their transport and they won't be able to get here in time to play the match. We're going to postpone it and hopefully get it in the fixture list for next month. You can all have the afternoon off—I'm sure you've got plenty of work to be getting on with."

As I got changed back into normal clothes, I had an excellent idea; I would use this unexpected opportunity to go to the town library to get on with the art project research. And then I remembered Joe's plan to come and help me and I wondered if I could find him to see if he was free. It didn't take a lot of thinking to work out that he would most likely be in one of the Art Rooms getting on with extra stuff he was doing in his spare Wednesday afternoons for the 'A' level.

I was right. As I walked across the courtyard to the old Art Block, I could make out his face through the window. He seemed to be in deep conversation with another student whose back was towards me and he hadn't noticed me making my way to the room.

"Joe," I exclaimed as I burst in through the door. "My netball match has been cancelled and I've had a great i…" And then I stopped. I clapped my hand across my mouth and took a step backwards. I felt air being pushed out from my lungs and I gasped at the sight in front of me.

Joe and Elsa Duke looked up. Embarrassed expressions on their faces told me I was the last person they wanted—or were expecting—to see. It appeared that my abrupt entrance had stopped them mid-flow in a very important looking talk together, just the two of them in a quiet room with no one else around and I could have laid a bet that the chief topic of their conversation was about me.

"Lizzy!" Joe exclaimed and went to stand up. Elsa sat still but gave me a look I couldn't fathom. "Lizzy," said Joe again. "Let me explain." But an explanation was not something I wanted, it would be an excuse anyway and I turned on my heels immediately and walked out of the room. No one—NO ONE—must see the look of horror and shock on my face. I ran to the girls' toilet and sat with my head in my hands. How dare he? How dare she? What was going on? Why now, and what signs had I missed? What on earth had I been doing for

61

these past six months chasing a dream which had just become a horrible nightmare?

I was utterly furious and incredibly hurt and I vowed then and there I would never speak to either of them again. I stopped sobbing and blew my nose hard and flushed the toilet to drown out any further noise—I didn't want anyone coming in to hear someone who had locked herself in a loo in such a state.

Then I thought; *I don't care. I'll show them. I can sort myself out,* and I remembered I still had the afternoon free and I would go to the library on my own and immerse myself in some research.

Luckily Mrs Atkinson was on desk duty and the library was very quiet. When I was eleven and twelve, I used to go to the library in the school holidays for their activities week and she recognised me and seemed pleased to see me. I was in a bit of a dishevelled state and Mrs Atkinson noticed how hot and bothered I appeared so she ushered me in to the empty Reading Room and asked if she could help. I explained about the art project giving it extra emphasis and importance and hoped she would think that I was just a bit stressed with all the work I had to do. We talked about the topic and she directed me to some journals and reference material and I knew I could easily spend an hour or so looking through them and making notes.

"We've actually got masses more in the basement," she said thoughtfully. "There are the archived newspapers from the '50s and they might have some good photographs. You know famous people in the headlines are always very conscious of what they wear as it gives off such an important image."

I thought this was a great idea and asked if it might be possible to see them.

"Members of the public aren't allowed in the basement and anyway there's so much stuff you wouldn't know where to start. But I tell you what, when I get a free moment, I'll go down and dig something out and put a bundle aside for you. Then you can see what I've found when you come again."

I thanked Mrs Atkinson and as she left the room to get back to the desk, I started to open some books. I needed to concentrate and let the turmoil of the previous hour drift away, but the image of Joe and Elsa sitting opposite each other apparently engaged in a private and meaningful conversation wouldn't leave my mind. It seemed utterly unfair and I couldn't imagine how naive and vulnerable I had become.

But some thought deep inside the recesses of my brain reminded me of my Mum's words of trusting when you believe something (or somebody) is right, and I couldn't completely let go of the belief that Joe was essentially a nice honest guy and clearly other people thought so too. Had I really failed at my first attempt to form a relationship? It was a horrid mystery and I felt thoroughly depressed, alone and let down.

Chapter Ten

Joe

I really didn't know what to do about the forthcoming Friday night youth club. Part of me wanted to be proud and show up and pretend that nothing had happened. I knew enough people there to have plenty of opportunity to chat and completely ignore Joe. And of course there was Amanda who I could take to one side and carry on our conversation from where we had left it the week before.

But another part of me didn't want to be anywhere near these folk. Somehow the hatred and anger I felt inside me didn't fit with the atmosphere and I felt I would be horribly out of place. So it was with many misgivings that I actually found myself walking up to the Rectory Rooms that evening. Once I got near the building I stopped. Something was willing me not to go in —not yet anyway. I wasn't ready to face people and I really didn't know how I might react when Joe looked at me, as I knew he would.

I was standing opposite the church and it was a building I had always liked and never found spooky. The daylight was fading but I guessed it would be unlocked and I thought I would slip in and sit for a while, gather my thoughts and be quiet.

I opened the heavy door, stepped inside and closed it quietly behind. It was an old church built in Norman times and had lovely carved bench ends on all the pews. The building smelt of polish and dead flowers and old books, but it wasn't a smell I minded. I crossed the aisle and decided I would sit in a pew and enjoy the last lights coming through the stained-glass windows. But to my astonishment I wasn't the only person to occupy the space. A hunched figure in an old blue woolly jumper was also staring out through the window. He had his feet on a 'kneeler' so that he could wrap his arms around his legs and he appeared to be completely oblivious of anything going on around him. I couldn't help myself—I quietly slid into the pew and sat next to him. He knew I was there but he didn't react. We sat in silence and somehow all the ancient whispered mutterings and footsteps through the centuries of that building entered into us and we sat contemplating the peace, solitude and serenity of the moment. It was a long time before either of us moved.

Finally, he broke the silence:

"Can you ever forgive me Lizzy?"

At that particular instance I wasn't entirely sure exactly what there was to forgive. Of course, I had rehearsed all sorts of insults and accusations I was going to throw at him, but this environment and reception weren't anything that had figured in my imagination and I was thrown off-course.

"I don't know, Joe," I said, with a big sigh.

"Elsa came to find me," he continued, lost in thought as if he hadn't heard my response. "She came to tell me she'd noticed us getting close and thought she ought to warn me that you were already going out with someone else."

I was almost beside myself practically standing up in my indignation.

"How **dare** …" I started, but Joe continued in the same thoughtful and deliberate manner.

"Of course I didn't believe her for one moment. But I couldn't understand why she was speaking to me like that. I hardly know her and yet she seemed so intent. So I began to tell her about this Youth Club and how I would see you every Friday evening—without a boyfriend of course—and then I went on to mention how very ill your Mum is. I'm so sorry, Lizzy. I know you didn't want it broadcast, but Amanda had a quiet word with me on the way home in the minibus last week and I just thought that it would do Elsa good to hear that you were struggling and that the last thing you needed was a false accusation."

I sat still and let his words mull around in my mind. As usual, I had jumped to conclusions and failed to appreciate his considerate and non-judgemental attitude. Yes, he had betrayed my confidence in telling Elsa about my home situation, but on the other hand he had defended me and wasn't prepared to accept any tale-telling from some third party. At that moment, I felt as if I loved Joe even more but despised Elsa Duke with greater ferocity than I had before.

"I really don't know what she has against you," Joe continued in his pondering style and thoughtful manner. "I was planning on getting to the bottom of it and finding out exactly what was what the issue, but unfortunately at that moment you burst in and broke up the party." I wasn't particularly sure it was a party I'd disturbed. It was an event that was going to lodge in my memory as one of the most humiliating moments of my life.

"I don't know," I said. "I really, really honestly don't know what she has against me. For the first two weeks of college, she was fine—quite friendly in fact—and then she just turned against me, big style, and it's been getting worse ever since."

"I've been thinking," Joe continued. "We mustn't let this come between us. I'm so sorry Lizzy. I've been so worried that you wouldn't come and if you did you wouldn't have wanted anything to do with me. Can you forgive me?"

"But Joe!" I exclaimed. "It's not your fault. Why are you blaming yourself? You've not done anything wrong." (I didn't mention the bit about my Mum). "I'm sorry too. I overreacted and as usual misjudged the situation—well I misjudged you—and I'm sorry. I'm sorry."

I shuffled a little closer so our shoulders and knees were touching and Joe put out his hand and held mine. We sat perfectly still gazing at the near-dark window. Time seemed to stand still. It's a cliché, I know, but it really seemed like that. Eventually, I shivered.

"We'd better go," said Joe. "They'll be wondering where I am." He looked at his watch. "Goodness Lizzy, it's nearly packing up time."

I couldn't believe it either. With luck, we'd just get to the Rectory Rooms before Dad came walking up the lane and I actually wasn't sure I was ready to start explaining this sort of thing to him.

Joe put his arm around me. "Let's make amends for our lost opportunity on Wednesday. How about we go to the library and do more of your research, I'd really like that." In fact, he said, "Why not tomorrow? I'm free as it happens."

"OK, well I am too," I considered. "The library is open on Saturday mornings. Yes Joe, I'd like that, let's do it."

So we linked arms and walked back to the Rectory Rooms, in the dark.

Chapter Eleven
The Revelation

Joe could walk to the library from his house (20 minutes) whereas I had to catch the bus from my village crossroads. Consequently, he was already standing outside the building waiting for me as I walked up the street. I could see he was smiling and wearing the same blue knitted jumper. He came towards me. A thought flashed through my mind that he wanted to kiss me but there were other people around us and maybe he thought it was still a little premature. Instead, he hesitated and held my hands.

"Sorry I'm late," I said.

Mrs Atkinson had kept to her word but she seemed busy and harassed.

"Oh Lizzy, I didn't think you'd be back so soon. I got Graham to bring some boxes up from the basement but I fear it's a bit of a mixed bag and I haven't had time to go through them yet. I rather think he picked some stuff at random. Anyway, whatever there is it's all from the mid to late fifties because that's when we first moved into this building. Please put back what you use in the same date order."

We assured her we would and Joe and I went into the Reading Room where, in a corner were stacked several boxes with a manila envelope on top marked 'FAO Miss E Morrison'.

"Well, there's plenty to get our teeth into," muttered Joe. "Goodness Lizzy, I'm glad I came to help." (So was I).

Actually the contents of the boxes weren't as onerous as we first thought. Basically, there were two piles of the town's weekly paper—*The Hillerton Herald*—from 1958 and 1959, and three bundles of *The Saturday Telegraph* from 1956 to 1959.

It was the latter which interested me more because these papers came with colour supplement magazines so there were plenty of pictures of outfits which I could sketch and make notes from. I got my paper and pens from the school bag I had brought with me. Joe was far more interested in the local newspapers, he of course was born in 1953 and some of the headlines were about various developments he could remember people talking about. He soon became quite engrossed and would quietly mutter the odd headline to me. I'm afraid I couldn't quite see what local politics had to do with my art project but I was pleased that he was so involved.

Thankfully there were very few people in the Reading Room. Everyone was supposed to be silent but we were tucked into a corner and the others (two gentlemen and one woman) were at the other end of the room and they all looked so elderly I thought they might be deaf.

For about 40 minutes I concentrated hard flicking through the magazines and writing lots of notes and making quick sketches. I certainly was going to have plenty of material. Joe was equally absorbed but he clearly wasn't the 'flicking type'. He would pick up each paper and study it carefully and quite methodically. As a result, he'd only got just over half-way through the first year in front of him—1958—when I heard him give out the most startled exclamation.

One of the Elderlies looked at us over his half-moon spectacles and said, "Sshh!"

The other two apparently hadn't heard, or had chosen to ignore us.

Joe looked at me with the most serious look and I couldn't for the life of me imagine what on earth he was making a noise about.

"Lizzy," he hissed slowly and choosing his words carefully. "Lizzy I'm here, right here."

"Of course you are," I whispered back. "Joe, whatever is the matter?"

He'd gone pale, the colour draining from his face and I could see his hand shaking on the paper as he passed it to me.

I put down the rather interesting magazine I was looking through and pushed my pad to one side, laid my pen on top of it and took the newspaper from him. I did not have to open it for the news I needed to read was on the front page; news that perhaps I should have been told of long ago; news that had stopped the world for two families and news that had somehow been overcome with the passing of time and the moving on of life with all its challenges and responsibilities. And as I read my heart gave a lurch. My pulse quickened and my breathing became shallow and I felt Joe's gaze never leaving my face.

Young Mums in Head-on Car Crash

Police and fire-crew were called to the scene of a bad accident yesterday at the cross roads of Hillerton Hill and Bemsberry Road.

The accident occurred at around 10.30 in the morning between a green Ford Station Wagon driven by Mrs Jennifer Morrison and a blue Austin A30 driven by Mrs Sheila Duke. The vehicles also had very young children on board.

Both women were rushed to St Margaret's Hospital.

It has been confirmed that Mrs Duke remains in a critical condition. Mrs Morrison suffered concussion and was released later in the evening.

Police at the scene stated that it was 'an absolute miracle' that the children survived with minor cuts and bruises.

Witnesses reported that the driver of the Station Wagon appeared to lose control towards the bottom of the hill and crashed into the Austin A30 which was waiting to cross the road.

A major investigation will follow.

Once again time for me was standing still. The Reading Room with its shelves of reference material and newsprint on large and solid wooden tables with the aroma of documents and peoples' body odours—for there are those whose greater priority is perhaps to read than to bathe; Saturday morning catching up with the press as the rest of the world rush by with their shopping. And two young people who knew each other a bit and were going to know each other a lot more sat together, and learnt of a secret they had just discovered; a secret which now made sense as if their eyes were open and now they could see.

"There has to be more," mouthed Joe. "More follow up. Stay still Lizzy, I'm going to find it—the Investigation," he added.

I didn't need to be told to sit still. If I had stood up my legs would have folded. I stared at the paper and read it again. And I read it again.

Why would I need to have been told? I would have been just two years and a few weeks old on the day of the accident. I was too young to remember anything. Yes, I knew my mother had been in a car accident and yes, I recalled her complaining of headaches, but a little girl growing up who is loved by her parents isn't going to worry because nothing traumatic that she recollects has happened. The memory wasn't kept alive by any physical manifestation and perhaps it was only the odd casual comment by a relative who might have observed, *of course Jennie, you'll still get headaches after that awful accident*, that might serve to lodge her condition in my mind.

Apart from that there was nothing. Two strangers colliding but never needing to meet again until thirteen years later the two miraculous little survivors happened to sit in the same History class.

"I've found it," Joe whispered emphatically and this time he put the paper between us so that we could read it together, taking our time; two friends sharing and absorbing a news item which was to have more of a profound effect than could ever be anticipated.

Once again I read it through several times slowly taking it in and coming to terms with all that it held in those few, short sentences.

The Hillerton Herald:
6 September 1958. Edition no:526

Local Woman 'Not to Blame' For Woman
Left Paralysed from Accident

An inquest into a near-fatal car accident on 25 July has
learnt that the cause was a major brake failure.

Mrs Morrison was driving a green Ford Station Wagon
provided by Watkins Garage. The inquest was told how she
had brought her own car in for minor repairs and had been
lent a service car for the morning. It was later revealed that
the Station Wagon was about to have new brakes fitted and
should never have left the premises. The mechanic in
question has since been dismissed from the company.

Mrs Morrison reported that, as she was coming down
Hillerton Hill she tried to stop and couldn't. At that moment,
the blue Austin A30 pulled forward and both vehicles
collided.

Mrs Duke, driver of the Austin A30 remains in hospital
having suffered spinal injury.

Mr Duke is suing Watkins Garage for gross negligence.

Commenting on the case Justice Carrington QC for the
defence stated that this was 'a most unfortunate accident'
and that he would take every effort to ensure that the law
would be changed and more rigorous checks made in respect
of Garage vehicles provided for customers.

Giles Fraser for the prosecution stated that a Station
Wagon was entirely the wrong sort of vehicle to be lent out
to a female driver.

I sat quite still and as I sat, I thought about Elsa Duke. She would have been nearly four, and a nearly four-year-old is developing memory. She would have remembered the event and she would have recalled the aftermath. All that she saw around her would have been kept alive by the reinforcement of debate and action. Everything about the situation would have stimulated a little girl's mind. A three-year-old girl looking forward to her fourth birthday—how grown up; a three-year old whose Mummy is taken away from her and put in a strange place for many weeks. A three-year old whose home becomes a different world as people talk in subdued tones and have serious expressions and who no longer dote on her—Elsa Duke—as they used to.

And when her Mummy eventually does come home, she is a different Mummy. She sits all day in a funny chair with horrible big wheels and she can no longer stoop down and pick up her little girl. Builders come in and change the house and now it is only Elsa who has to go upstairs to her bedroom at night, and she doesn't like it.

Why can't she have her old Mummy back? And what has happened to her Daddy who has become so quiet and miserable?

And so she grows up. She starts primary school and she makes friends—but all her friends have normal Mummies and they stare at hers. And then she goes to secondary school and she does some more growing up and makes different friends and life gets better and she learns to cope. Then, she starts sixth form and goes to the local college where she will study for her 'A' Levels and take one extra 'O' level.

She talks to her Mum in the evenings and they always discuss her day. And one day in late September 1971 after two

76

weeks at her new college she tells her about the History lessons and her Mum casually asks the names of her classmates. It's just an ordinary conversation happening around the country in households where parents take an active interest in their son's and daughter's education. And Elsa, who has grown up nurturing a seed of anger which will one day spill over and consume her thoughts and actions, who knows that she will get retribution when she finds out who was responsible for changing her life and causing untold misery, just happens to say to her Mum: "There's a girl in my History group from another school. She's quite nice. Everyone calls her Lizzy. But her real name is Elizabeth Morrison."

* * * * * * * * * * *

Joe seems to have gained a bit of composure while I sit lost in my reverie and he becomes practical and decisive. "We must make a copy of these articles," he says. I am about to protest but there is more 'shushing' from the other incumbents so I simply nod in acquiescence.

"I'm sure the library has a photo-stat machine," he whispers, "I'll go and ask and then I think we'd better find somewhere to have a coffee."

The three elderlies look up and glare at us.

I glance at Joe numbly and he gestures to the pile of papers in front of us to put them back in order and I dutifully do as I am commanded. Just as I am finishing, he returns with two white sheets of A4 paper along with the two newspaper editions and these we slip back in date order into the right bundles. No one would ever know.

I take the two copies he had made and use the empty envelope marked 'FAO Miss E Morrison' to put them inside. Then I put the whole thing in my bag with my notes and pens. We quietly push our chairs under the table and leave the Reading Room. Mrs Atkinson was nowhere to be seen but I just about have the presence of mind to say thank you to another member of staff and to please pass on the message.

And then we step outside.

* * * * * * * * * *

We sit opposite each other in Hillerton's new Wimpy Bar. Joe has a coffee and I have a milkshake because I feel in need of something cool and sweet.

"What an absolutely, completely, utterly ridiculous comment that man made," said Joe.

I wasn't sure what he was referring to I said nothing.

"I mean it makes not the slightest bit of difference—male or female—who is driving the vehicle if there are no brakes. Idiot."

"Maybe there was nothing else he could say," I mused. "Anyway, what exactly is a Ford Station Wagon and what does an A30 look like?"

"It would have been the Works vehicle," Joe replied. "The sort that a garage needs for towing cars that have broken down. It would have been quite a hefty beast imported from America whereas a little Austin…that's just a small family car. Quite frankly, Mrs Duke wouldn't have stood a chance with that thing crashing into her and I suppose she had no warning whereas your Mum might have had a few moments at least to brace herself." I shuddered and thought how different things could have been; for me, for my Mum and for Elsa Duke and her Mum.

"If she hadn't hit the Austin she would have gone into that high river wall," said Joe grimly as he pictured the road layout in his mind.

"But you know it was an accident. Your Mum was exonerated—cleared—so it wasn't anyone's fault except the mechanic and I wouldn't mind betting he was made a scapegoat. Someone higher up in that garage gave the all-clear and wasn't going to admit it."

I sat hunched over the table with my hands around the tall cold glass and sucked up the remaining froth of the milkshake through my straw. I probably made rather disgusting bubbling noises but Joe didn't seem to notice and was continuing with his logical line of thought.

"Your father is a Solicitor and he's not just any solicitor. Everyone speaks highly of him. I haven't told you this Lizzy, but when my Grandma died two years ago there was a real problem with her will. Mum went to your dad's firm and she says he was brilliant. Actually, that's partly why I knew it was Elsa telling lies the other day because I was so sure you'd be taking after your dad for integrity."

I blushed somewhat but I believed Joe to be right. My father's company were the best in town and a lot of that was down to his hard work and his reputation as a lawyer.

"Your Dad would only have been a junior partner back then when the accident happened," Joe continued as if he were putting pieces of a jigsaw together. "But he would have known good people—people who were extremely professional at what they did. I wonder, I wonder if the Duke family felt they were at a disadvantage."

"But surely," I started to protest but Joe kept going and put his hands around mine speaking earnestly.

"I'm not trying to suggest anything untoward, it's just that it was an accident that was proved beyond doubt and I bet we could find more written work to support it, so why can't the Duke family let it rest? Or do you think they harbour a grudge because, well because, your dad knows the ins and outs of the legal system?"

"And they don't," I finished.

We were quiet; each of us lost in our own thoughts wondering to what extent Joe's theory was plausible. I had little knowledge about the Courts but enough to appreciate that a QC (meaning Queen's Counsel) was a very senior Barrister.

Eventually Joe looked at his watch. "I'd love to stay all afternoon with you Lizzy, but I need to get home, changed and ready for work. I go to the Rose and Crown on a Saturday and they like me to be there early to do the veg prep and then it's full on with taking orders and waiting at the tables." He sounded apologetic.

"I need to get back too," I said, "Don't worry I've only got twenty minutes before my next bus."

And even though it was in the wrong direction which meant Joe would have to rush and perhaps be later than intended, he came with me to the bus stop and waited.

On the way home on the bus I thought about his words: "I would love to spend all afternoon with you, Lizzy."

So would I. With him.

But the big Elsa Event was pervading my thoughts and possibly his too. What should I do? Who was it who said *with knowledge comes power*? I didn't know and I certainly didn't feel powerful. I felt sad at finally knowing why Elsa hated me in the extreme and vicious way she did and I thought of another quote, this time I knew where it was from: *Ye shall know the truth and the truth shall set you free.* I now knew the truth but that didn't make me feel free either. I couldn't see how anything could be resolved except perhaps that when I was on the receiving end of one of Elsa's attacks I could at least understand where she was coming from.

Eventually I allowed my pragmatic approach to take over and I did a mental calculation: there was one more week of the spring term left and then we would have a fortnight off for the Easter holidays. The summer term would resume in mid-April (I couldn't remember the exact date but I knew there was a Parents Evening in the first week back—that was when our art project had to go on display). Then it would be May and revision time for exams so with any luck we would only have about four weeks at the most of History left.

That therefore meant approximately eight more sessions with Elsa if I managed to avoid her for the rest of the time. We would both be back at college the following September but that would only be for one year and then Elsa, I assumed, would be off to university. I knew the subjects she was doing for A levels and she would be in the second year of her sixth form whereas I would be in the first. Hopefully, I would hardly ever see her so I reckoned all I had to do was to hang on in there till June. **June!** Goodness that was only just over two months away—how on earth could I be worrying about Elsa Duke when my own mother's life might be hanging in the balance?

All these ideas were running through my head as I got off the bus and walked home. It was a Saturday afternoon in March and although there was a keen wind, the sun was shining. Late snowdrops had given way to primroses and the banks on either side of the lane looked colourful and pretty. We lived in such a quiet area of the village and there was very little traffic. No pavements of course, and certainly no street lights. I loved the countryside even though I slightly envied Joe for being able to walk into town and not need to wait around for buses or try to catch a lift when you wanted to be somewhere.

I was so lost in my thoughts as I pushed open the side gate and walked up the path to the back door that I didn't take in the fact my mother was kneeling down, trowel in hand and pulling up some weeds—my mother! I couldn't remember the last time I'd seen her outside doing this, maybe last September?

"Oh Lizzy, there you are," she said and stood up slowly. "I was hoping you'd be back soon. I should have stopped a while ago but I thought I would keep going and wait until you returned and we could have a cup of tea together, but now I think I may have rather overdone it." She stood for a moment before taking any steps.

"I'll go and put the kettle on," I said. "And we'll have a sit down and a chat."

"That would be lovely—oh, and Lizzy, Dad got some nice biscuits when he did the shopping. Let's have one of those too."

We sat at the kitchen table and Mum cradled her mug of tea and drank slowly. She did look worn out and it must have been the most energetic day she'd had for months. Finally, she started to explain.

"There's been a bit of good news…"

I then remembered it was just over a week ago that Dad and I had walked back from Youth Club and he had told me there was to be the appointment with Mr Hargreaves during the week. So caught up was I with the Elsa/Joe/ Art Room drama that I had forgotten their appointment had also been on that same dreadful Wednesday.

"The blood tests were better than expected and Mr Hargreaves is keen to operate. Lizzy, I want you to know the operation is not guaranteed and it does come with risks. It's a new procedure and I could be in hospital for ten days. The thing is, I've got a bit stronger lately and that means I stand a better chance of recovery if they operate and even if the operation is successful and they remove all the nasty bits it could all come back. We mustn't get our hopes up too much."

I sat drinking my tea and munching a biscuit and thought about my brave Mum. She didn't usually talk too much about her condition and generally waited for me to do the prompting. But this time it was different—she had some news and it was tentatively good and she wanted to share it. So much so, she had kept going outside waiting for me and wanting to talk. My lovely, lovely Mum.

"So when would the operation be?" I asked.

"We don't have a definite date, but it's looking likely to be just after Easter. I know that's quite soon—two to three weeks. I've got to keep going and build up my strength even more."

"Oh Mum, you must do what you think is right."

"I know and I have been thinking about it since Wednesday. But you can cope for a week or two without me and Dad will be OK and anyway you can come in and visit. Well, I jolly well hope you will!"

Mum's mind was made up. She would go ahead. Of course she would. She had a strong character and was a determined person. Once she had made up her mind to do something she would always carry it through to completion, perhaps that's why she had been such an inspiring Sports Coach and a supportive Teaching Adviser.

I thought of Joe at that moment getting on with his shift at the pub and I had an idea:

"Tell me what's for dinner tonight and I'll do all the cooking. I fancy doing some veg prep."

I took my bag upstairs—the bag that contained the envelope and the envelope that held the secret but now was not the time to bring it up. I couldn't help thinking, however, as I peeled the potatoes that I, as a fifteen-year-old, would shortly have my Mummy in a hospital. How would I feel about it all? Would I be welcoming her home afterwards to a new and better life? Did I believe that this might happen and could it actually be possible?

Chapter Twelve
Chris

In a drowsy state the following morning it was a great relief to realise that it was Sunday and I would have the whole day to think about things and spend some more time with Mum. Would I tell her about the newspaper articles that were safely stowed away inside my bag? I hadn't made up my mind about that. I wanted to tell her a bit more about Joe but if I started recounting our time in the library and then in the Wimpy Bar I wasn't sure what I could include and what I could leave out of the conversation. Finally, I decided she had enough on her mind at the moment and I didn't need to resurrect the past and give her more unhappiness to dwell on.

There was something else rumbling around in the back of my brain and I struggled to identify it—was there someone else who I knew that might be in a spot of bother? Then I remembered that two weekends ago I had gone to see Auntie Cath and she'd had an Intruder. I wondered if I ought to pay her a visit and just check she hadn't had any more unwelcome visitors.

After eating some breakfast and checking if it was OK to go out for the morning, I set off across the fields to her rather run-down cottage.

It was as if she were expecting me when, just as I was raising my hand to knock, the door opened and she invited me in. Spoodles greeted me with a great amount of tail wagging.

"Come in. Come in. Wet boots on the newspaper please. Coffee?"

I took up my normal seat by the stove on the wooden stool opposite hers and Spoodles lay between us on the floor in front of the fire.

"So what have you been up to and how is Jennie?"

I concentrated on the second part of her question and elaborated on my Mum's condition telling her about the gardening, the blood test results and the forthcoming operation. I knew Mum would like Auntie Cath to know.

Catherine Van der Hayde was not one to gossip or spread rumours. Despite generally knowing everyone's name locally (villages are like that) she was very discreet. People knew very little about her and I have to say that I felt even if I told Auntie Cath my innermost secrets or fears she would listen intently, demonstrate that she was understanding and be committed to complete confidentiality. I think that's why Mum was very happy for me to give her regular updates because she knew they would go no further.

She listened and nodded until I had finished and then drained the rest of the coffee from her mug. She looked directly at me:

"And how is Chris coping?" she asked unexpectedly, but perceptibly.

If truth be told I was avoiding all thought about Dad for I knew deep down that he was shouldering all the stress and worry and making a huge effort keep things going. He had looked awfully tired in these past few weeks and there was little I could do. He was working hard in the office as well. I could tell he was busy and he would bring home extra files to look at in the evenings. Once or twice after Mum had gone up to bed early, I would find him asleep on the sofa—his papers still spread out on the coffee table. He was looking a bit thin as well but I really didn't feel I could cope with Parent Number Two to worry about on top of everything else. I suppose I had just hoped he would manage because he was the sort of person who never gave in.

"Well," I said taking a deep breath. "I think he's worried about Mum and he's working hard and doing extra cooking and shopping."

"And all the household chores as well no doubt," retorted Auntie Cath. "Although I'm sure you do your bit Lizzy."

She was right. Dad was doing a lot in the house and whilst I did do some jobs, I could probably do more. I felt a little uneasy, changed the subject and said that I hoped she hadn't had any more intruders (by the way).

Never one to be interrupted from her train of thought Auntie Cath replied that she hadn't. But some link in her consciousness with my question and the main topic of conversation gave rise to her next comment:

"And of course, your father's office—what a wonderful reputation he's built up over the years. I've been so impressed with the reports I've heard." She stopped short and became a little abrupt, "I mean everyone knows what a good firm it is," she added quickly as if to steer me away from making any personal connection she may have inferred.

Not wanting to press her and give her a cause to regret her words I simply said,

"Well, I hope you're locking your door now."

"Oh yes," she replied. "I am, whenever I go out."

"And—at night?"

She looked at me with incredulity:

"Lock it at night? Good Heavens! Why ever would I want to do that?"

Chapter Thirteen

Incentive

It was the last week of the spring term and all I had to do was to get through Monday morning's double History and one single period of History last lesson on a Tuesday afternoon and then no more Elsa Duke until after Easter. There was always the chance I might bump into her elsewhere during the week but I was determined I would keep a good lookout—if I could avoid her that would be a good thing. Elsa did Art with Joe but there was nothing I could do about that and anyway I completely trusted Joe now. Thinking about the art made me realise that the last time Elsa saw me was when I rushed out of the room on the previous Wednesday afternoon—what a lot had happened since then!

Mr Cook was in a very energetic mood impressing upon us how important it would be to *start revision early* and *what a good opportunity it would be* to get going over the two weeks of the Easter break. No one really grumbled or resisted as he had that knack of making you feel you wanted to try hard. There was also a bit of an incentive. Tradition was that he always took his star students on a History trip after the exams were over. It was something of a yearly highlight in the academic calendar. Of course all his students were stars and no pupils got left out.

Along with giving us various topics to revise he also began to mention *by way of encouragement* the end of term outing.

"You've all been such a good group this year," he began. "I'm hoping we can push the boat out and do something extra special. I'm not making any promises but *it might* I repeat *might* involve a trip to London, and *possibly*, I repeat *possibly* involve an overnight stay." (Much rumbling of approval around the room). He continued, "Given the fact it would take about three hours to get to 'where I am thinking of going', it would be nice to set off the evening before and then we can have the whole day to explore 'where I am thinking of going'. (More nods and positive expressions). Mr Cook had a way in which you felt you were all part of his conspiracy and he was drawing you in with his humorous approach as the absent-minded professor, but I think he deliberately acted up that a bit. He was nothing if not astute.

"However," he continued playing to audience participation. "There's always a downside in life," and at this he gestured to get us all to groan: "The Powers That Be say there is no money in the kitty and if we want to go, we have to find the money ourselves. I'm dead against asking parents to chip in because some can afford it and some can't. I can quote lessons from history, Dear Friends, we don't want an Uprising on our hands. So I'm suggesting that, along with your revision, you have a good think over the holidays and see if you can come up with any first class, highly lucrative fundraising ideas. You may like to work in small groups or just on your own—up to you—but I will be looking for suggestions next term." He made a few more pithy comments about not wanting to turn us into venture making capitalists but nevertheless expecting us to make a tidy sum and then he turned to the subject matter of our lesson.

I felt Elsa's eyes were on me rather a lot but I was determined not to look at her. I wondered what had been said between her and Joe after I had rushed out of the room. It seemed from what Joe had inferred that he'd probably brought the discussion to a rather abrupt end and I considered that Elsa might be thinking she'd misjudged Joe's reaction.

The one thing of course that she would not have a clue about was the fact that I now knew the cause of her pure hatred and anger towards me. How different would it be if she knew I knew? It was no good surmising and once again I was letting my thoughts drift when I should be concentrating. I would rather think of nicer things such as when I would next see Joe.

This thought was bothering me a bit because I wondered how that might happen. I knew I could find him in the Art Block but that meant running the risk of bumping into Elsa. Likewise, I knew I would see him in the Maths lesson but learning about the equilateral sides of a triangle when we were sitting (very close) to each other was one thing and having a deep and meaningful conversation together was another. Thankfully Joe had already thought through this and slid a note to me when we were sitting in our Geometry lesson that afternoon. I surreptitiously opened it inside my textbook: *Busy today. Sorry. How about tomorrow at lunchtime in the Library? (Not the one in town of course!)* I gestured with a 'thumbs up' sign when our teacher wasn't looking but he was.

Chapter Fourteen

Discussion

We met at the entrance to the library and we were both early.

It was a sunny day and neither of us wanted to be indoors: *let's go and sit outside*, so we sat down together on a wooden bench at the entrance of the Visitor's Car Park.

For a while we sat saying very little, both of us enjoying the fact we were together with no one else around. Finally, Joe enquired, "How was History yesterday?" (By that he meant how was Elsa Duke behaving to me in History yesterday?)

Actually, it was fine and then I asked him how was the Art lesson that morning? (By that I meant how was Elsa Duke behaving towards him in Art this morning?) and apparently, she was OK. I was getting a little put-out; here we were in this special moment together and the chief topic of conversation once again was about my sworn enemy and not about us. Joe was silent, deep in thought.

"You know, I've been thinking," he said slowly choosing his words carefully. "You're probably not going to like this but I think you need to forgive her—for her actions I mean."

I was completely taken aback.

"Forgive her? Why should I be the one to forgive Elsa Duke when it's her that's done everything horrible to me?" I nearly exploded.

"I know," he replied. "But I've done a lot of thinking since I saw you off at the bus stop. I know you don't need to forgive her and I know you haven't done anything wrong and I know that if you do forgive her—in your heart and mind that is—it might not change the way she behaves to you because of course you're not able to sit down and have a conversation with her, as things stand at the moment. But somehow I feel if you forgive her for all the horrible ways she has treated you then I think you might be letting something go."

I was really quite stirred up by Joe and his comments. He had not spent the last six months on the receiving end of insults and anger towards him. He did not know what it was like to wake up in the morning thinking of the day ahead and then realise with a sickening dread that he was going to be sitting in the same room as Elsa Duke. It was really quite unbelievable that he should be telling me to forgive and let go when all the evidence showed that it should be Elsa saying sorry to me and walking away from her vindictive behaviour.

The last thing I wanted was a row with Joe, he did not understand how I felt even though he was sympathetic, and with a huge effort to keep back the indignant tears which were welling up I said, "Joe I've got a lot on my plate at the moment. Mum is probably going to have a risky and serious operation." At that I did start to sob a little, perhaps some tears of self-pity but also because Joe's was a rather nice shoulder to lean on. Life seemed rather unfair to me and I had every right and reason to cry, but I was also aware of a little thought deep in the recesses of my mind that it was this unfairness which was actually bringing us together enabling us to be sitting in the sun with me sniffing into his jumper.

He put his arm around me and I felt even more protected and lucky. Eventually, he looked at his watch and said he had to be getting back to the Art Block. I had lessons to go to too.

"I'll see you soon Lizzy, but I've been meaning to tell you I've got a really busy couple of weeks coming up. I've got to get all my artwork in for assessment and on top of that Sue Paynter has asked me to a special display for the Parents Evening. Over the holidays I've got extra on at the pub because their busy season is just starting up. I might not even be able to make it to Youth Club this Friday if they are too short staffed. Maybe if we can't see each other I can ring you in the holidays."

I had mixed feelings—seeing Joe in the flesh would be much more preferable to the odd phone call but it was nice he had been thinking ahead and didn't want me to feel he was staying away deliberately. I told him my number; in those days a three-digit phone number was easy to remember! We reluctantly got up from the bench. Yet another afternoon that we knew we would love to spend together: 'Joe and Lizzy'. If only.

Chapter Fifteen

Easter

So began the start of the Easter holidays. It had been a long term and I was looking forward to a bit of peace and quieter moments with Mum. It was nice to feel the time was mine and I had no major commitments or places to rush off to and in fact that is exactly how the first week progressed. The weather was reasonable for April, there were some bright but cool sunny days and the evenings were getting lighter. Mum and I would like to sit and chat without turning the lights on and watch the sky grow dark. Perhaps we had got used to the dim light during January.

I also got on with the art project and took over the dining room table with all my notes and sketches spread out in front of me. Mum got very interested and I'm sure it helped to distract her from her illness. She was born in 1930 and was therefore exactly 20 years old when the 1950s decade began. She had been quite a follower of the fashion trends even if she couldn't afford the latest designs and clothing.

"I used to make all my dresses and spend hours with the old Singer sewing machine," she said laughing. "Goodness we wouldn't really think about that today." She dug out her old photo albums which contained a lot of her and Dad's wedding photographs (1954) and their subsequent honeymoon in Wales. Then there were pictures of me as a baby (1956) growing up as a toddler wearing a rather appalling assortment of knitwear.

We laughed a lot and giggled at the old pictures which even though they were only taken two decades previously seemed terribly old-fashioned and 'make do'.

"You have to remember 1950 was only five years after the war had ended," Mum considered. "There was still rationing when we got married and life was quite tough. We never thought we would be able to afford a car but of course Dad was working hard and earning money and eventually when you came along, we bought an old Rover. But it was an ancient old thing and more often than not in the Garage being mended." (I said nothing). Then Mum still thinking about my art project had a brilliant idea. She remembered she still had a drawer full of old dress and knitting patterns. (Goodness knows why she kept them—people did in those days: *never throw anything away, you don't know when it might come in useful* was a well-known saying and typical of the times).

I helped her sort through the drawer and carried down an assorted bundle of goodies—wonderful as it happened because some contained photographs and there was always a clear picture of the outfit on the front of the pattern which was easy to sketch. I was in my element and completely absorbed.

These were good days with Mum. Despite the fact that the forthcoming operation was looming and we were still waiting for a date I was spending quality time with her. I would do a bit of housework after breakfast before sitting at the dining room table and then in the afternoons help with preparing dinner. When she was particularly tired and uncomfortable I would do it all. At some point we would cuddle up on the sofa with a hot drink, not necessarily saying much but happy to be together, very much aware that life can change and change quite quickly and that the important thing was to value what we had right at that moment.

Dad was working hard but my extra support around the house did not go unmissed and he too appreciated my company and contribution. Much later we would often do the washing up together after dinner. By then Mum would have gone upstairs and it would be just the two of us in the kitchen. Dad was tired, terribly tired, and I knew he was so worried waiting for the big event to happen. And after the 'Big Event'? What then? What would be the outcome? The waiting seemed to be the most difficult for him; the man who always found a way of fighting through solutions and getting results. So it was a big relief to us on the first Thursday of the holidays when a letter came through the post with a date for her hospital operation. It was to be in exactly two weeks' time (the same date of the Parents Evening as it happened).

* * * * * * * * * *

According to the calendar we were in what the Church called 'Holy Week', a time that I always associated with Easter eggs but of course for Christians there is more to it than just chocolate. A nice little event happened on that Good Friday morning—I had a phone call from Joe. He was at work and on his coffee break or, as he put it 'in-between the dirty dishes'. He was ringing from the pay phone in the pub and every so often the pips would go and he had to feed in more coins. It was a somewhat disjointed conversation partly because of the interruptions but mainly because we were both so excited about talking to each other we didn't really know what to say. It seemed a waste of time to be discussing mundane matters (like the weather) and there were long pauses and then after hesitating we'd both start speaking at the same time.

Finally, Joe said that he was running out of money and had to get back to the washing up, "I don't think I'll be able to make it this evening Lizzy, it's a day off for lots of people and it will be extra busy here but I have got the Bank Holiday Monday off. Keep the day free because we're all going to have a riot on the hills. Wear old clothes."

When I returned to the dining room (our phone was fixed to the wall in the hall) Mum noticed my flushed face and rather excited body language. She looked at me with a knowing expression and smiled, "He seems nice this Joe of yours. I hope I'll meet him one day." I hoped so too, but I wasn't sure when and how, and was he really 'My Joe'?

* * * * * * * * * *

That evening at Youth Club I found out what The Riot was all about. Apparently, it was an Easter tradition 'we all'— that is Youth Club members and parents who could offer lifts and any other hangers-on—decamped to the hills for a Wide Game on the Bank Holiday Monday followed by a campfire supper. It sounded fun but exactly what a Wide Game was I had yet to find out.

Being Good Friday, it was a solemn and rather challenging religious spot that night. To my surprise it was taken by Amanda. She spoke about losing her Mum (which was exactly a year ago) and how her faith had helped her to deal with the grief. She spoke about love and forgiveness and how important it had been for her to let things go. Then she went on to talk about a man called Jesus dying on a cross on all those centuries ago and how a new way was opened up to God. I thought I knew the Christian story and for weeks now I had been hearing testimonies from people whose lives had been changed as a result of their new-found faith. But tonight it was different. It didn't wash over me and I listened intently and felt rather strongly someone was giving me a particularly personal message about love and forgiveness.

It occurred to me that I needed to give this some serious attention.

Chapter Sixteen

Wise Words

Sitting on Auntie Cath's kitchen stool the next morning I still had the previous evening's thoughts turning around in my head. Two weeks had elapsed since I had last paid her a visit and she was very pleased to see me.

"Now I need to ask you an important question but before I do, tell me—how is Jennie?"

We talked a bit about my Mum and I was able to give her the date of the operation.

"Of course she will actually be going into hospital a couple of days before that so they can do some final checks and get her ready," I added.

Auntie Cath was quiet and thoughtful, "Hmm," she uttered and then looked at me intently: "And how are you Lizzy May? How are **you** coping with all this and everything that is going on in your life?"

Intuitive as ever, she had a knack of getting straight to the point and for the first time I felt myself voicing recent thoughts that had been running through my mind that I hadn't yet been able to articulate. I made a hesitant start.

"I'm not really sure…" I answered finding myself unable to reciprocate her direct and rather piercing eye contact, and instead looked down into my coffee cup.

"I made a discovery…and found out the reason why someone—a girl at college absolutely detests me. It means that I know why she hates me but that will not alter the fact that she will still keep being horrible to me. But now I know, I kind of understand. Her mum is in a wheelchair and with my mum being ill I'm sort of seeing why she is so vindictive towards me. You see there is a reason why she can blame me even though the event that put her mum in the wheelchair could never have been my fault. It's actually been eating me up a bit and I dread seeing her.

"One day it got so bad she tried to come between me and a guy I've got to know and told him a horrible lie about me. Fortunately, he knew it wasn't true. I don't really know how to deal with it all. Part of me wants to get my own back and do something nasty to her and part of me, well part of me is beginning to understand bad things can happen in life as well as good things and it's how you deal with them that matters. And that's where the religious bit comes in as I've been going to that Church Youth Club in the village since January and there's been a lot of talk about love and forgiveness. All to do with God, I suppose," I added.

It was a long speech and I wasn't sure how I was sounding and if I was making any sense but Catherine Van der Hayde sat quite still and didn't speak for a long time. She seemed to be struggling to tell me something—something rather important that she might not have told many other people in her life.

Finally she looked at me with an earnest and serious look.

"Firstly Lizzy May, you must find your own way with a faith. Do not let anyone persuade you to believe in something if you are not comfortable with it. You are a free spirit and you are able to work things out for yourself and reach your own conclusions. Some people like to be told what to believe and I can tell you that there are many out there who like to tell others what to believe, how to think, and how to live. If you take that to the extreme it is called Suppression and that never did anyone any good—look at the Nazis. But you are not someone who needs to be told what to believe and you must never, *never* be coerced into doing that." (Here she was quite emphatic). "But thankfully we are not talking about extremists here and I'm sure your Youth Club has well-meaning people in it who only want the best for you and who feel that they need to share the faith they themselves have experienced, so that is good.

"There have been two occasions particularly," she continued thoughtfully, "When I have been in a very tight spot and considered my cry for help was answered. The more recent one was when I fell off that ladder. I lay there and knew that someone would come along and find me. The first time was a rescue of a different sort, well…maybe that's a story for another time." She had lost the intense look and there was a more faraway expression on her face as if she was recalling an event that happened a long time ago. Then she recovered and became a little brusque again.

"But secondly, Lizzy, you have been given a wonderful opportunity to re-evaluate your life; Jennie's illness, this business with the girl and now your discussions about faith and forgiveness and letting go. It's all happening to you when you are still young and you have choices you can make. Not everyone gets that moment, that moment when you need to stand still and think things through and recognise that the paths you decide on will affect the rest of your life. Some people don't re-evaluate their lives until they are middle-aged, and some people never do."

We sat quietly with the clock ticking behind us and Spoodles giving the occasional grunt. There was a lot to take in, a conversation between a searching 15-year-old girl and a wise woman in her 50s who seemed to have lived another life. It was a conversation which would take me on a journey and it was a memorable moment.

I looked up and glanced into the sitting room which was looking uncharacteristically tidy as if Auntie Cath had been having a serious purge on her paperwork.

"By the way, what was the question you wanted me to remind you about?"

"Oh yes," she replied, getting up and moving to the sink. "Something to think about and check with Jennie and Chris please? I need to go away for a few days and wondered if it might be possible for you to look after Spoodles for me. I know you have a cat but I dare say they'll *cope,*" and with that she gave her dog a hard stare. "I won't be going before Jenny's op and I don't want to put any extra pressure on you all so please ask them to think about it. If necessary, I can put Spoodles in a kennel but I'd rather not."

I would be only too delighted to have her dog and I was sure it would be OK. I promised I would ask and let her know the answer.

"Are you going anywhere nice Auntie Cath?"

She looked thoughtful. "Not really," and gave a sigh. "Something I should have attended to years ago. Sometimes you have to do the wrong thing for it to be right."

I put on my boots and coat and left to be back for lunch. How extraordinary, she was a remarkable lady and a very special friend, but what an odd comment to make as I was leaving. How on earth could something wrong, be right?

* * * * * * * * * *

When I got home someone had pushed an invitation through our letter box.

Easter Monday 1972

St Stephen's Church Youth Club invites you to:

A Wide Game—great fun to be had by all on the Bantock Hills. Come dressed in old clothes and footwear for running in. (Bring warm clothes for the evening).

Pick-up by mini-bus or private car 11.30 am outside the Rectory Rooms.

Please bring a packed lunch—squash will be provided.

You are also invited to a camp-fire supper for which parents are welcome too.

You will be dropped back at your home when the evening finishes. A contribution of 20p towards the supper would be appreciated!

"What's a Wide Game?" asked Dad curiously, looking at the note.

"I haven't a clue, but when I find out I'll let you know!"

Chapter Seventeen
The Wide Game

Monday morning saw me standing outside the Rectory Rooms at 11:20 dressed in old jeans and a T-shirt with a jumper tied around my waist and plimsolls on my feet. I had 20p in my pocket and some sandwiches in a paper bag.

The minibus came along with Joe in the front seat and an empty space next to him. Had he reserved it? He jumped out. "Good to see you Lizzy." He was looking happy and relaxed and I was rather thrilled to see him.

There was some general discussion and conferring between parents and Keith about lifts and who was going with whom and eventually we set off to the hills in convoy with about five cars following the minibus.

We arrived at the rendezvous and were to be split into two teams called The Bandits and The Vagabonds—the latter quickly to become known as The Vags. I suppose there would have been about fifteen teenagers in each team and some of the more athletic (and brave) parents also volunteered to join in.

Keith spread a large Ordnance Survey map on the bonnet of the bus and said, "Right gather around everyone and let me explain." He drew a large circle with a pencil near some woods and a second circle a few inches to the right of the map near another wooded area. "These are going to be the two bases," he announced.

"Bandits are to the east and the Vags are to the west. When you are in your own base you are safe and no one is allowed to get you. Between your bases is open country. The aim of the game is to capture as many opponents as you can. Bandits will wear a yellow string around their wrists and Vags will wear a red one. Andy is the captain of the Bandits and Steve is captain of the Vags. Choose your teams please captains!" It turned out that Joe was chosen by the Bandits and I was selected for the Vags.

Keith had a few more things to say: "I'm now going to walk each team to show them their bases and then you'll all know the way back to the car park. This is where we will eat our picnics and have our campfire supper later so we will come back here for lunch before we start. Just a reminder of the rules; you capture your opponents by taking the coloured string from their wrists—no violence please. If there is an accident I'll be here by the minibus and your team captains will each have a whistle and someone will need to send a runner for help. Whatever happens you all need to be back here by four o' clock. Look out for one another and work together as a team."

The Vags sat down and ate their lunches while the Bandits were shown to their base. Then they returned and the opposite happened. We were each given a coloured piece of wool which Amanda tied around our wrists and at about one forty-five we made our way to our respective bases.

For the next two hours I lived what I can only describe as one of the most exhilarating and hilarious times I have ever had in all my fifteen years. I absolutely revelled in the sheer energy of it all and the ludicrous way in which after about ten minutes the whole thing turned into utter chaos. I ran about like a mad animal screaming and shouting and having the best fun I'd had for a long time. I was out in the fresh air with the wind in my hair and the sun on my face in beautiful country in a wide-open space.

Perhaps it was the fact that for months I had been holding myself together for Mum, shielding myself against Elsa, and willing myself to appear controlled in front of Joe, but for the first time in ages I let go. I capered about and charged into enemy territory and captured a Bandit before anyone else. As the game developed, we all became a bit extreme and the rules went by the board and the Vags lived up to their name of being absolute vagabonds. The Bandits were doing pretty well too. We had a hilarious time and there was the heightened state of excited anticipation when someone pounced on you from a discrete vantage point; much shrieking and plenty of physical interaction as we all resisted the taking of our precious wrist wool.

I still hadn't been captured by 3:30 and was on the point of running back to base and then returning to the car park when I heard a noise behind me. I was in a small copse and not far from the Bandit camp. I'd got separated from the little group I was with and so there was no one to cover for me. Just then there was the snap of a twig and I saw Joe from the corner of my eye. I ran like crazy back to safety but knew he was behind me and gaining. The adrenaline poured through me and I became faster than I knew possible charging across the open moors jumping tussocks of moss and ducking under any low hanging branches as I got closer to base. I was laughing and my heart was pounding and I felt alive—ALIVE—the joy of the energy and swiftness that I had. I tumbled into my base just as Joe caught up. He made a grab for me and missed and fell straight into the Enemy Territory. We rolled around and laughed and tears of ecstasy ran down my face.

"You can't catch me!" I said, breathless and triumphant.

"Oh yes I can Lizzy. But not today."

We made our way in a group back to the car park and flopped down on to benches, tired but incredibly happy. What was it about being out in the fresh air in a big open space with masses of friends and having sheer fun and using up energy as if it were an inexhaustible supply?

And so we came to supper, hot dogs and burgers cooked on the campfire by Amanda aided by some of the parents. We sat in a circle and stuffed ourselves with food and the sun started to go down. I felt more relaxed than I had been for ages. I'd been running all afternoon shrieking like a wild animal and behaving like the absolute epitome of a vagabond. Something that had been eating into me had been extinguished and I felt joyous and calm inside. It was a wonderful moment.

Steve and Andy the two captains were also the guys who played the guitars so when the eating was over they struck up and we sang songs and choruses around the campfire. Then we had a visitor, the Vicar of the village church who was called Reverend Duncan (I wasn't sure that this was his first name or his surname) stood up and spoke to us all.

He reminded us of the Easter story but this time his focus was on the empty grave and the Resurrection. He told us about two disciples walking on the road to Emmaus and the risen Christ drawing near and talking to them although they didn't recognise him at first. And then he spoke about that same Christ appearing to the eleven apostles who were fearful and behind locked doors, and saying to them: Peace be with you.

I listened to what he had to say and somehow the words were full of meaning to me. Was I in need of some peaceful reassurance?

Auntie Cath's words had been churning through my thoughts too and there and then I made a promise to myself. I had a week before the start of term and I would use some of that time to do some serious 're-evaluating' as she put it. I would wait for the right moment when I was on my own and in the most suitable place.

Rev Duncan—everyone seemed to just call him Duncan—stopped speaking and Steve and Andy got up to play the last song. I didn't know it but it was an easy tune and in four/four time so it's sort of stuck in my brain as a haunting melody. The song could be sung in harmony or as a round and we sang it several times:

Seek ye first the kingdom of God, and his righteousness; and all these things shall be added unto you.

(Then there was a chorus of Hallelujah in the same lilting tune).

Ask, and it shall be given unto you; seek and ye shall find; knock, and the door shall be opened unto you. (The chorus was then repeated).

I sat and took in the words. I was seeking but I wasn't sure exactly what I was looking for. And maybe I was knocking at a door waiting for it to be opened by someone who I could quiz with some serious questions and get the answers I needed. And what was it about all these things being added to you? What things?

I was sitting next to Joe and I shivered and, before I knew it, he ran to the minibus and got his coat and draped it over my shoulders.

I felt as if I wanted this moment to last forever—the glowing embers of the campfire and all the friendly faces sitting around it, the lovely feeling of exhaustion following an afternoon of activity seeping through my body; the questions that I would find answers to and the wonderful boy who was sitting next to me and who had just given me his coat.

I was happier than I had been for months and I knew that I, Miss Lizzy May Morrison, was going to take up that gift that was being offered up to me—that gift of re-evaluating my life and making decisions that would send me forward on my road for all the remaining years I was given to live on this planet.

I was dropped back at home from another car at ten to nine.

The house was quiet. A note on the table:

We've both gone to bed, early night. Please lock the door. Hope you have had a good day, see you in the morning—Love M and D.

I dumped my empty bag of lunch things in the kitchen bin, locked the door and turned out the light, went upstairs to the loo and brushed my teeth. I took off my clothes and dropped them in a pile where I was standing then I put on my nighty and tumbled into bed. It was 9pm exactly and I was about to have the best night's sleep I'd had for months.

Chapter Eighteen

Promises

Mum came into my room and drew back my curtains.

"You're late this morning, Lizzy." I looked at my watch and saw it was 8 o' clock. Goodness, I'd slept for 11 hours! She sat down on the edge of my bed,

"Did you have a good time yesterday?"

I propped myself up on my pillow, I was aching a little from the sheer pounding I'd given my muscles.

"It was absolutely wonderful," I replied already smiling as the images of the previous afternoon came flooding into my mind.

"I ran everywhere and it was hilarious—such fun." Then I went on to tell her all about The Bandits and The Vags and the rules as I understood them although I was still a little hazy feeling sure that a certain amount of anarchy and confusion had developed not long into the game.

Mum listened to my account and she was so pleased to see me happy and cheerful and energised. But there were shadows on her face which told me a story of the pain she was enduring and how the thought of spending all afternoon running over hills and through woods was like some distant dream for her; my mother who used to be so fit and active could no longer walk up the stairs without having to stop at some point and regain strength to carry on. If there had been a way of somehow extracting energy capsules from my body and donating them to her, I would have done so, right then and there.

* * * * * * * * * *

I was of course in the second and final week of the holidays. I had a certain amount of History revision and the art project to finish and one or two other subjects to do work on so the remaining weekdays progressed and I was fairly engrossed in my work around the house and keeping up my special times with Mum.

I also remembered Auntie Cath's request to ask if we could look after Spoodles when she was away. I mentioned this to Mum carefully choosing my moment when she seemed a little brighter. Mum considered; the thought of walking a dog was the most unlikely thing she would ever be able to do, but she had a lot of time and respect for Catherine Van der Hayde and didn't want to let her down.

"If you promise to do it all yourself, I suppose it's OK, but he'll have to be in the laundry room with his food and bed. I don't want to see Tootsie doing a runner."

I said that would be fine and that I'd tell Auntie Cath.

At the back of my mind was the big re-evaluating promise I'd given myself and somehow I knew I was putting it off, letting my revision take over and not allowing myself sufficient time or space to attend to my resolution.

In the end, I decided I would wait until Friday evening and speak to Amanda about it at the Youth Club.

But as I walked up the lane to the Rectory Rooms on my own that evening Auntie Cath's words came back to me: "You are a free spirit Lizzy May." She was right; I had an independent nature and I also didn't need anyone to interfere or influence my special moment. It would be my decision and I wanted to do it on my own. I ambled into the bar and saw Joe lifting up boxes of confectionery onto the counter for Amanda.

"Hello you," he said.

I took a bit of a gulp and addressed them both:

"I'm actually not going to stay tonight…I need to do something…I'm going to find a quiet place on my own and think through a few things but," I added, "I might be back before packing up time."

And even though I was desperate to be with Joe and maybe play table tennis, and sit with him and chat and help Amanda, I turned and left before I or anyone else could change my mind.

It was cool, and although April was getting on and the evenings much lighter I shivered a little and decided that being somewhere quiet outside was not going to be the ideal spot. So I turned back to the church and lifted the heavy door handle and went inside. It felt right to sit in the same pew that Joe and I had sat in exactly four weeks earlier. What a lot had happened since then! I glanced around and looked out of the colourful stained-glass window, this time there was greater light coming through and it seemed even more beautiful. Then something else on the wall caught my eye which I hadn't noticed before. It was a carved wooden plaque donated by someone many years ago for it had an *In Loving Memory* inscription at the bottom and a date in Roman numerals of *MCMXX*, but it was the actual words on the plaque which absorbed my attention:

Seek ye first the kingdom of God and all these things will be added onto you.

This was part of the song we had sung around the campfire and I realised now that they were verses to be found in the New Testament bit of the Bible.

I sat for a long time and read the words through and contemplated. It seemed as though the remaining moments I had on my own in the church that evening was going to be rather important and I wasn't entirely sure how to progress.

Eventually I started talking out loud:

"I'd like a door to open and for things to happen, and to find out if it's really true that if I ask for things they will be given to me—the right things that is. I guess for that to happen I have to seek first of all the Kingdom of God whatever that means. But I would kind of like to find out more and be part of it all. And there are things I want to happen that I'm very, very worried about. So, I'm asking for my Mum to be all right when she goes in for her operation, and I'm asking for Dad to be OK and be able to cope and not get ill himself, and I'm asking for Elsa Duke to be happier and to let go of all her nastiness and anger. And," I added, "To please let things be good between me and Joe."

I sat in the silence and felt a lot more peaceful but it occurred to me there was something else to do, so taking a very deep breath I continued: "I'm sorry for Elsa and her Mum. I'm sorry about the accident even though it wasn't my fault or my Mum's. I understand why she's so bitter towards me but I forgive her. And if it means I've got to put up with it for a few more weeks or months then that's OK. I can do it. I do forgive her."

I thought of other people in my life, Auntie Cath and her Intruder and Frankie with her boyfriend Dave, and it seemed as if I was bringing all the people that mattered to me to a door that was opening in front and letting me through. What was on the other side? I didn't know but at that moment I felt as if I was seeing my world as I'd never seen it before—a world that had enormous potential to be utterly beautiful and full of goodness and life and laughter and happiness. And I saw a world with a darker side—one with anger and pain and suffering as if there was a Presence who wanted to seek out and destroy anything that might be good and life-affirming. It was an extraordinary moment but I actually felt I was beginning to glimpse something rather deep and spiritual; that my eyes were more open and someone was hearing my prayers and wanting to draw near to walk along with me— just like in that bit about the road to Emmaus.

There were no hallelujah choruses and no one to clap me on the back and say *wow*. I didn't want anyone else to spoil the moment. Who was God? I didn't know, but it seemed as if he knew me. I supposed that had I been a fifteen-year-old girl in another far-off land I might be sitting in a very different place of worship looking at other types of inscriptions on the wall, but that appeared unimportant too.

I lingered for a few more moments and then decided I would get back in time to say hello again and then goodbye, but as I stood up, I had an incredible feeling that something had been lifted from me. I had forgiven Elsa Duke and in a most peculiar and unexpected way it felt as if I had been forgiven too.

I made my way back to the Rectory Rooms where the packing-up process was in full swing. This was the first evening Dad had relented and said it was now light enough me to walk back on my own, but as it happened, I wasn't going to do it solo. Joe came straight up to me and glanced at the wall clock.

"There's about ten minutes before the minibus leaves, let me walk five minutes with you down the lane and then I'll run back for my lift."

So that's exactly what we did and believe me we said nothing all the way. We walked hand in hand and when it got to the point where we had to separate, we dropped hands and I went on and Joe turned back. But it has been the silence of those moments, just walking together that were so special. Nothing needed to be said because Joe had guessed what I had done and it seemed to me that he had completely understood.

Part Two

Summer Term 1972

Chapter Nineteen
The Parent's Evening

It would be nice to report that there was a dramatic improvement in the Lizzy/Elsa department but Monday's first History lesson at the start of the summer term did not inspire me with hope.

Mr Cook, refreshed from two week's holiday, was back with renewed energy and determination to get us all *up to speed* and *ready for the off* as he put it, referring to the forthcoming exams, and "not to forget that fund-raising activity."

We had just about finished the syllabus and every so often he would fire quick revision questions at us.

"Right listen up everybody, who can tell me—what was the name of the last battle to be fought on English soil?"

I put my hand up straight away,

"It was the Battle of Sedgemoor."

"That's good Lizzy, that's good—I wonder for a bonus of five points can you also give me the date?"

I thought: "Er…was it 1686?"

"Oh nearly, but not quite."

Else's hand. "1685," she said.

"Well done Elsa. Well done." And I felt Elsa's big smirk reach right across the classroom for her little moment of victory and plant itself squarely in a deprecating way on my head.

But never mind as I had plenty of other things to think about. I had decided in my lunch break I would nip across to the shops and get a card and a little gift for Mum as she would be going into hospital the next day. I went into Woolworths and hunted for the right sort of card, somehow *Get Well Soon* didn't seem the most appropriate message and in the end I simply opted for a plain card with pretty flowers and a 'No Message Inside'. Then I chose some nice smelling lavender soap, a lilac-coloured flannel and some lavender talcum powder—at least it was all on a similar theme.

When I got home that evening, I found some flowery paper and I tied up each item separately so that it would take her longer to unwrap, then I wrote in the card. I thought about putting something like 'thinking of you', but couldn't bring myself, so in the end I just wrote: *To Mummy. I love you. Lizzy*.

I put everything back in the shopping bag they'd come in and tiptoed into her bedroom and put the whole parcel onto the top of the suitcase she had been packing to take with her.

* * * * * * * * * *

Dad had the following morning off work as he was due to take Mum to the hospital for 11 o'clock. As I left for my bus, there was not a lot I felt I could say, so I gave her a hug and squeezed her as tight as I dared and put my head on her shoulder: "I love you Mum," I said again, this time out loud.

"My darling Lizzy," said my brave mother, "Don't you worry about me, I'm in safe hands. They'll get me ready for the operation on Thursday, and by Friday I should be through the worst of it. Come and visit me at the weekend, and don't forget to look after your father." She added this with a weak smile.

Wednesday came and went with little to report. Mrs Paynter was getting in a bit of a tizzy about the art display for the parents evening and, because I knew that Dad could pick me up late on Thursday on his way back from hospital, I offered to help. She was very appreciative. As a matter of fact, I was rather proud of my final piece having spent so many hours on it and I was secretly pleased that I would have the honour of displaying it—hopefully in a prominent position.

I saw Joe but he was also extremely busy and had more or less confined himself to the Art Block whenever he could (a place which I was trying to avoid). Consequently, our time together was minimal. We had a few moments on our own after our Maths lesson.

"I'm thinking of your Mum so much, I'm sure it will go OK."

I thanked him and then spent a few moments being furious with myself for wishing he'd said he was thinking about me so much.

"I won't be around to help at the Parents Evening, either Lizzy," he told me, "Work wants me. At least I'm earning money to help me with university next year."

My heart gave a little lurch when I realised that 'next year' meant this coming September and he would be moving away. Would anything go right for me?

123

Thursday, the day of Mum's operation arrived and as I got out of bed, I dressed with a heavy heart wondering what the day would bring and how we—all three of the Morrison's—would get through.

I wasn't the only one to have things on my mind that day, Isaac Chombele, the Caretaker, nearly flattened me as I came around the corridor and he was rushing the other way.

"Lizzy, so sorry. So sorry!" He looked hot and flustered.

It became apparent that he had to get everything ready for the Parents Evening. By 'everything' this meant the chairs and tables put out in the hall, the class rooms cleaned and organised and refreshments for the parents set out.

"I've already moved the reception table three times to different places and now it's back in the first position. I wish Damien Green would make up his mind." (Mr Green was the new college Principal and he insisted that everyone, staff as well as students, should call him by his Christian name).

I liked Isaac a lot and felt sorry for him. Typical that he was taking the brunt of someone else's mismanagement.

After lessons finished, I went into the hall with Mrs Paynter and helped her to put up the artwork. Big display boards had been erected (by Isaac of course) and all we had to do was work out what looked best and where. I had a good eye for colour and balance and soon the display was looking extremely impressive.

When it was finished, we stood back and admired the spectacle—Joe's work was absolutely stunning. You could be forgiven for thinking you'd walked into an Art Gallery and not a college hall.

I was just thinking that I might take a break when Isaac rushed in with an armful of flowers. If I thought he'd looked harassed at nine that morning this was nothing compared with how he looked now.

"He's done it again this **Damien** of ours. Right at the last moment I get a call from the Principal's Office. *Isaac, we need a floral display just pop and get some flowers, will you?* I don't know Miss Lizzy. I'm good at most things but a flower dresser I am not."

I smiled inwardly at the potential double-meaning of his statement but I wasn't going to explain.

"Here Isaac," I said. "I'm free, give them to me. I love flower-arranging."

With an enormous sigh of relief, he handed over all the bunches and showed me where a large vase was sitting on a pedestal—empty, and waiting to be filled.

For the next half hour I had some of the most enjoyable moments of the day. Something about the scent and the physical act of arranging the stems was relaxing and therapeutic. Finally, when I stepped back to look at the end result, I had to admit, it did look rather splendid.

There were a few students who had offered to help and we were hanging around just before the parents started to arrive. Miss Russell came into the hall and saw us and said "Gosh you lot, has no one given you a drink?" Apparently the 'no one' hadn't had the foresight to plan ahead for the helpers. She happened to have a key for the serving-hatch (fringe-benefit of being a PE teacher and needing to sort out refreshments for after-hours matches). We gratefully had a cold drink and a couple of biscuits.

It was 6.30 and parents started arriving and making their way to the various subject stations where the relevant tutor was seated—that is after they had admired the art work which you couldn't fail to miss.

I no longer had anything to do and the display was to stay up for another few days so it wasn't as if I was needed for dismantling.

I ambled off to the entrance and leaned against a pillar and watched people coming in and wondered about Mum and how much longer I would have to wait for Dad to come and get me.

It was then, out of the corner of my eye, that I noticed something entering through the door. I glanced up idly, looked away and then became alert as something big and unusual focussed my attention and I looked more closely. And as I stood alone from my vantage point leaning against the pillar I watched a self-propelled wheelchair with a woman in it and, beside her, a man of about the same age as Dad making their way slowly into the hall. There was no mistaking them: Mr and Mrs Duke. And **nothing** had prepared me for the sight I was about to behold.

If I was expecting Elsa's mother to be a poor wretched woman, skin and bones, harbouring a deep and bitter resentment and sunk into the abyss of a wheelchair I couldn't have been more mistaken. She was alive and animated and pointed excitedly to the exhibition as soon as she entered the room—Elsa's work was displayed as well of course. I stared at Mrs Duke who looked radiant. She was pretty and she was wearing a lovely bright jacket over a stylish looking blouse. Her hair was beautifully done and what little make-up she wore was just enough to enhance her already good looks. Mrs Paynter recognised her and came up and soon the pair were smiling and laughing and then Mr Duke joined in and they spent ages looking at everyone's artwork and admiring it.

I stood still and stared.

And then the absolute irony of the situation hit me like a hammer walloping into my chest. Here was Mrs Duke in the picture of perfect health (albeit in a wheelchair) and meanwhile my Mum was in a hospital bed having a serious and potentially life-threatening operation. Here were Mr and Mrs Duke attending their daughter's parents evening as they had done for every year of her education and would continue to do so, taking an active interest in everything she did. And there was I hanging around for Dad who himself was exhausted and nearly sick with all the stress. This was the first Parents Evening they'd never attended for me and I wondered with a sudden sickening dread if they might ever make it to another one together.

It was all too much. I was tired out and distraught. I got my college bag and went outside to sit on the same bench Joe and I had used so that I could keep an eye open for our car. It was cool and there was a smell of cigarette smoke wafting through the air as I sat down, pulled my knees up to my chest and heaved huge sobs of exhaustion and despair.

"Hey Miss Lizzy. Miss Lizzy. What's up?" Isaac's voice. His evening was not yet done but for the moment at least he could step outside and have a smoke. (He wasn't supposed to do that).

"What's up Miss Lizzy?" he asked in his lovely deep, sonorous voice. He took a big drag on his cigarette and as he blew out said, "I'm not supposed to be doing this."

Sometimes a conversation can happen between two people regardless of their differences—a conversation which will have profound consequences even though the pair might not know it at the time. Despite our completely polarised backgrounds, age and status we sat like two friends; one prepared to talk and the other willing to listen.

I told him all about my Mum and the operation she was having that day. I told him Elsa Duke hated me and how I'd just seen Mrs Duke in a wheelchair in the picture of health and accompanied by her husband. And I told him I was jealous because Elsa's parents were at the evening and mine couldn't be.

He listened and he nodded and he let the ash burn all the way down his cigarette without even glancing to tap it off. Then I was quiet.

"Oh Miss Lizzy, I'm sorry for your Mum and I'm sorry there's someone out there that doesn't like you—that's never good for anyone."

Then he paused, "Forgive me Miss Lizzy, but there's something I don't understand. Why are you so upset about seeing Mrs Duke so well and happy and what's that Elsa got against you that's something so big?"

I looked down and opened my college bag and rummaged to the bottom of it. I pulled out the crumpled manila envelope and silently handed it to Isaac.

"For Attention of Miss E Morrison," he read out slowly. "What's this Lizzy?"

"Read it," I said. "It will explain everything, and," (I added) "as far as I'm concerned, you can keep the contents. I'm not sure I want them back." I shut my bag. "Thank you Isaac. My Dad's coming now so I've got to go. Thank you for listening."

"And thank you for doing them flowers. I don't know what I'd have done without you. You've been my little life-saver today."

He put the envelope in his pocket and I got up and walked towards our car.

Before I could ask—

"She's had her operation and they're keeping her in Intensive Care tonight."

He looked grey.

We said little as we drove home.

"Have you eaten?"

I told him I'd had a cup of orange juice and a biscuit earlier and I guessed that was more than he'd had.

"Shops are shut now and there's not much in the house,"—almost too tired to care.

But an astonishing act of kindness had been placed at our kitchen door step in the form of a box with a card on the top:

To Mr Morrison and Lizzy. We are thinking of you. With love from all your friends at St Stephen's Church Youth Club. Hope you enjoy!

We carried the box to the kitchen table. Inside lay a savoury flan topped with grated cheese and smelling divine.

Next to that was the most calorific looking chocolate cake you could possibly imagine. We didn't bother with forks and spoons. We cut two huge slices of the flan and ate it with our fingers. Then we had two enormous helpings of the cake washed down with a couple of glasses of milk. When we could eat no more, Dad locked up, I fed Tootsie and we went to bed.

Chapter Twenty
Frankie

I woke late after a disturbed night with my head aching, my throat sore and my body telling me to forget about feeling well for the next few days. I went down stairs in my dressing gown, flopped onto a kitchen chair and put my head in my arms on the table.

"Hmm looks like you're going down with something. I'm not surprised. You've had a lot on your plate Lizzy, but please don't give it to me. Someone's got to stay fit in this house and it better not just be the cat!"

I gave a feeble smile and said I would lie on the sofa. Dad told me he would give college a ring, pop to the office and wait for the hospital to let him know when he could visit.

"It might not be till the afternoon. I think you should stay put. No one will want your germs where Mum is."

Quite frankly I hadn't the slightest intention of going anywhere.

I lay on the sofa. Tootsie joined me purring loudly delighted with the company. Occasionally I would lift up my hand to stroke her and that took an effort.

At two o' clock Dad phoned to tell me Mum was now back on the ward and he was going to see her. "I might be back late," he said a little apologetically.

"Don't worry, I'll be fine. Give Mum my love."

But fine, I wasn't and by 4 p.m. after I'd looked at the clock for the umpteenth time all I wanted was for someone to get me a drink and stroke my hot head—or fevered brow—to be more poetic.

Half past four and the phone rang. I struggled into the hall expecting Dad's voice again but to my astonishment it was Frankie. She sounded breathless.

"Hey Lizzy, are you alright? Only Alice said you weren't on the bus last night and you weren't on it this morning or coming home today. You alright?" She repeated.

I told her I was on my own and full of germs and that I'd helped with Parents Evening the night before; that Mum was in hospital having her operation and that Dad was visiting her and I was at home. I had a sore throat and an aching head and couldn't go anywhere.

"Oh, Love," said Frankie. "Hang on and I'll be down."

"But I'm…," I started to say. Too late, she'd rung off.

True to her word, within twenty minutes there was a tap at the door and in walked Frankie holding a carrier bag. She went straight to the sofa and gave me a hug.

"Frankie, you'll catch something!"

"Me, nah, never. Anyway," she retorted, "It'd take more than a silly sore throat to put me out of action."

I felt like saying that this wasn't just a silly sore throat and wait till she had it with a raging temperature and feeling absolutely rubbish but I refrained and instead said,

"How come you're on your own, where's Dave?"

"Finished with him," she declared, "Should've done it weeks ago. In fact I should never have gone out with him in the first place."

"Oh Frankie—I'm sorry, tell me about it."

"Nothing much to tell." At this, she delved into the carrier bag and brought out a bottle of Lucozade.

"Mum doesn't know I took this," she admitted. "She always keeps a bottle handy in case one of us lot gets ill. She hides it in the back of the cupboard. No one knows it's there 'cept me. But she won't mind if she knows I've given it to you." She went and fetched two large glasses from the kitchen, and poured a medium one for me and a generous one for herself. The bottle had got shaken up in the bag so it fizzed out all down the neck and left orange splodges over the polished coffee table. I took a grateful sip, it was warm and sugary.

"He was too controlling—always wanted to know where I was and what I was doing. At first, I quite liked it. You know, someone checking up on you, asking what you're up to. I thought it showed he cared. But it wasn't that at all. He couldn't cope if he thought I was out enjoying myself with my friends if he had to stay in and babysit. In the end he said he didn't want me going to the Youth Club without him, but when I asked him to come along too, he said it wasn't the sort of thing for him. So we were both missing out.

"Anyway, it all came to a head last week. I told him I would be going away for two nights on our Duke of Edinburgh Expedition and he said he didn't want me to go. He said we were a couple and we shouldn't be doing things without each other, **meaning** I shouldn't have any fun on my own. When I told Mum I no longer wanted to go (I made some

133

excuse) she exploded and said she and Dad had already paid for the trip.

"And then she said *if I find out it's that boyfriend of yours behind this…*Well, it got me thinking and I sort of woke up, opened my eyes. And I realised just how much fun he was leaching out of me and how much I had been looking forward to the trip so that I would be on my own, with my friends and not with him. So that was it. I'm done with boys now. I'm not having another one."

"Oh Frankie."

"Nah, don't you worry about me. I'm all right."

But I could see she'd learnt a lesson the hard way for with mistakes comes experience, and with experience comes—well—maybe a better relationship in the future. Frankie wouldn't be without a boyfriend for long, of that I was sure. But she would be more careful and the next time it would be based on trust; trusting each other and giving independence and finding the joy in shared friendships and activities.

We drank Lucozade.

"Anyway, come on, Miss Dark Horse Lizzy, what's this I hear about you and Joe? Come on, spill the beans, tell me all."

"There's not much to tell. We…like each other a lot…and we've done a lot of…talking." I suddenly felt incredibly naive and feeble compared with my worldly friend.

Frankie giggled. "That's not what I mean, Stupid. Tell me all. What's it like when he kisses you?"

"We haven't actually kissed yet," a blushing face, deeper red than my already flushed fever.

Frankie choked on her drink. More fizz to wipe up.

"You haven't kissed, and you've known him how long, what planet is he on?"

My turn to snigger now, my lovely friend Frankie—the two of us sitting on the sofa sharing boyfriend stories as far in the extreme as possible and yet such a closeness between us.

"Don't worry Frankie. I'll let you know when he does."

We both started laughing and then she had to go. I was exhausted.

I was asleep when Dad got in later. He was kneeling by the sofa and I woke to feel his cool hand on my hot forehead.

"Hmm, not a lot to pick and choose between you."

Poor Dad—two down and one to go.

"Do you want anything to eat?" I shook my head. My throat felt dry and my mouth was furry.

"I think I'll brush my teeth and go to bed."

"I'll have the last of the flan and a bit of cake in that case," said Dad. He went to get up, "What's all this sticky brown stuff on the table?"

"Frankie came and brought Lucozade and we spilt a bit. I'll clear it up tomorrow." (Although at that moment I felt that it would be weeks before I felt strong enough to lift a dishcloth).

Saturday, Sunday, Monday, Tuesday. Dad would go and visit Mum in the afternoons and Frankie would come and see me. She made sure I ate something. The first day all I wanted was a small bowl of cereal. On Sunday she made cheese on toast and on the following two days she came with two different types of soup which she bought on her way back from school. Monday was Heinz Tomato and Tuesday was

Crosse and Blackwell's Cream of Chicken. If she hadn't brought the food on a tray to me on the sofa, I'm not sure I would have bothered to eat. Where would I have been without these visits and her cheerful disposition and matter-of-fact-attitude?

Mostly she would talk and I would listen.

She told me more about 'Dysfunctional Dave' (although he **was** good-looking and had a nice body) and about her big family and what they were up to, stuff she was doing at school and the D of E Expedition she would be doing at the end of the following week.

"I'm happier than I've been for months," she announced, "I've got my life back."

I imagined Frankie in a few years' time. I had no doubt that she would eventually find someone who was just right for her—someone who was utterly devoted and strong enough and patient enough to let her make her own decisions even if he had to pick up the pieces afterwards. They would have a house full of kids; theirs and everyone else's and there would be a kind of chaotic hospitality offered to anyone who came knocking at the door. She was the sort of delightfully spontaneous woman who, upon discovering she was expecting their fourth child, would shrug and say something like *how did that happen then*?

By Wednesday I was starting to feel less like a wrung-out rag and more me. By all accounts Mum was beginning to get a little stronger too. How would she have managed without all those visits from the one who loved her most?

136

Frankie turned up that evening with a Shepherd's Pie. "Mum made this for you and Mr Morrison. She said when you've finished it, please can she have her dish back?"

On Thursday there was some news. All being well Mum would be home the next day. Maybe it was the thought of her homecoming that spurred me into action or perhaps the nasty germ had had its fling and decided to move on because I suddenly felt as if I had more energy and wanted to do things. I vacuumed the living room including all the cat hairs from the sofa. Then I went outside and picked a big bunch of flowers to place on the newly polished coffee table. It was the first week of May and our roses were starting to bloom and I made a nice arrangement with a few bits of greenery added for effect here and there.

On Friday morning I walked up to the village shop and bought ingredients to make a strawberry trifle and some salmon sandwiches—that is, tinned strawberries and tinned salmon—1972 style! These were two of Mum's favourites (not together of course).

I felt a bit guilty I hadn't got back to Auntie Cath about having Spoodles, so at lunchtime I phoned her to explain that I hadn't been well and that Mum was coming out of hospital. She seemed a bit distracted.

"Lizzy, I'm so glad you've rung. Things have escalated a bit and I need to go away sooner than I had expected. Would it be too much trouble for you to have Spoodles on Wednesday week? That is in twelve days' time. I'll be away until the following Friday."

I said I was sure that would be fine and I'd walk straight up after college on that Wednesday evening and pick up her dog.

"That's a weight off my mind. Thank you so much." And she rang off rather abruptly.

It was later in the afternoon when I heard our car draw up on the drive and I rushed out.

"Oh Mum I've missed you **so much** and I'm so, so sorry I got ill and couldn't visit."

"My darling Lizzy. I've missed you too and I've been worried about you." She was tired and weak of course; she'd had major invasive surgery and it would take her months to get over it and get some strength back. Meanwhile—the results? We would have another two to three weeks of not yet knowing, but I sensed there was already a bit of a change, maybe that which was so rotten and nasty inside had been taken away for good?

It was a quiet weekend and at long last I got on with some revision. We were a family unit—the Morrison's—together again under one roof. Dad hadn't caught my bug and maybe, just maybe, life might be returning to normal.

Chapter Twenty-One

Isaac

Monday morning and my bus was late. I just made it into History while Mr Cook was halfway through the register (handy for me). I settled into my normal seat.

It was while I was getting my books out that I sensed something was different. Was someone missing? No, we were all present and correct. Had someone got a different haircut or changed places? There was something decidedly odd happening in the room. And then I glimpsed at what appeared to be the strangest mirage—Elsa Duke was smiling. She wasn't just smiling generally around the room; she was deliberately aiming it in my direction.

Mr Cook, efficient as always and keen to set the pace, began by asking us about the fundraising assignment, but his first comment was directed at me.

"Ah Lizzy, glad to see you're back, hope you've not passed the Black Death on to anyone else?" I assured him I was fine and no, I hadn't. He continued:

"We talked about our ideas last week and I believe I'm right in saying most of you are in groups making a start on your plans? But what about you Lizzy—have you come up with a multi-million pound award winning scheme?"

As a matter of fact, I had given it some thought and my idea was probably based on a combination of helping Amanda at the bar and knowing about Joe's job in the pub.

"Well, I was wondering about setting up a Sandwich Station at lunch times," I started. "I thought we could have some tables out in the foyer and buy bread, butter and different fillings then we could make up sandwiches to order as people were waiting. Maybe we could do a cold drink and charge one all-in price. I don't think it would upset the canteen staff," I added. "It would only be for a week or two and we wouldn't be doing hot food."

There were various mutterings of approval around the room. This time I felt Elsa's beams were positively bearing down on me.

"Excellent idea, excellent Lizzy, now I'm wondering who would be willing to assist in this culinary venture?"

Elsa's hand shot up.

"I will Mr Cook. I was going to help Emma and her team with the hand-printed note paper but there's four of them already and I'm sure they can manage without me. You don't mind Em, do you?"

Mr Cook gave me a curious look, "Excellent," he repeated. "Happy with that, Lizzy?"

The moment history was over I dashed out of the classroom—the first to leave. I had a fifteen-minute break before my next lesson. I tore across to the Art Block to find Joe who was just about to help Isaac carry a newly varnished table into the art room.

"Lizzy, good to see you, are you better and how's your Mum?"

I went straight to the point.

"Something's happened to Elsa, she's smiling at me and when Mr Cook asked who wanted to work with me, she was the first to put up her hand."

Joe was as mystified as I was, "Nothing to do with me, although come to think of it she was very pleasant and chatty to me at the end of last week."

Isaac put down the table and looked at me.

"Isaac!" I said aghast, "You've told her. You showed her the articles."

"No Miss Lizzy," Isaac replied in his deep solemn voice as if a little hurt. "No Miss Lizzy. That's your story and that wouldn't be right. That's not mine to share." He paused.

"But when she was doing her project and I was cleaning these tables here we got to chattering. I was still working you see. And as I was sanding off these old marks and stains well, I started to tell her *My Story*. There's not that many I tell it to these days because it brings back some of the old fears. And it's not everyone who should hear it either. But for one or two that maybe do need to hear, it makes a difference. It's a story of loss and a lot of hate and a long, long time to heal up and let go; to forgive and make things better.

"By the way," he added, fishing into one of the many pockets of his overalls, "I've been carrying this around for over a week. Time to give it back." And he handed me the familiar brown envelope.

I ran back to my next lesson and sat perfectly still pretending to concentrate but my mind was racing.

Elsa had also heard a message of forgiveness and letting go. It was a story with far more loss and consequences than she had experienced and it was told to her first-hand by someone who you couldn't fail to respect and trust.

And Elsa, being an intelligent and sensible girl, went away and did a lot of thinking. At some stage, she woke up to the fact that what was eating away inside her was really not worth it and probably not conducive to her future well-being either. She had a lovely Mum and a great Dad and what was the point of her life if she spent it chasing an old vendetta which no longer seemed of such immense importance?

Chapter Twenty-Two

The Date

For both Frankie and I, the weekend couldn't come soon enough. Frankie was eagerly preparing for the Expedition and I was looking forward to Friday night's Youth Club. I hadn't attended a normal session for four weeks and there was a lot of catching up to do. Firstly, there was a big thank you to make (mainly to Amanda) for the wonderful box of food left on our doorstep and secondly—and most importantly—I was keen to spend some quality time with Joe. The odd moment we had seen each other at college had been rushed and frequently interrupted.

Everyone wanted to know how Mum was and although I didn't have much in the way of specific information at least I was able to explain that she'd had her operation and was now at home and doing well. Joe seemed to be somewhat distracted as if he had something on his mind. We played a couple of games of Table Tennis and I won both comfortably. Then he put his bat on the table;

"It's hot in here, can we go outside for a bit?"

We slipped out with no-one noticing and walked along the lane until we came to a gateway where we stopped. Joe leaned against the stile. He appeared to be surprisingly uncertain and was struggling to say something in the right way. Eventually:

"Um, I was wondering if you would like to come and see *A Clockwork Orange* with me? It's on tomorrow, as it happens, at Hillerton's Odeon. And then I wondered about going to the Wimpy Bar again. I know we've been before but that was different. It would have to be a matinee showing—for the film I mean—because I'm afraid I've got work in the evening."

I looked at Joe, surprised at his uncharacteristic reticence and then I guessed:

"You're…asking me out on a date?"

"Well, yes." He laughed a little nervously and then looked immensely relieved, "Yes Lizzy. I suppose I am."

We stood looking at each other, the light growing dimmer, and a new moon appearing above the trees and then we both did what we had been wanting to do for a long time—only perhaps up till then the moment hadn't been right. We drew back and looked at each other and smiled. A little shy. And then we did it again.

Frankie would have approved.

* * * * * * * * * *

Midday, and I met Joe at the appointed place. A big hug, too public for anything else, but that didn't matter. I hadn't walked back down the road the previous evening, I had **danced**—happy, swinging my arms and jumping about like a mad thing in the middle of the lane.

"Come on," said Joe. "Let's go and join the queue, it was starting to form when I came past a few minutes ago."

We rounded the corner but in a matter of moments the queue had swelled to three times its size. Joe put his hand to his head. "Oh Lizzy, I've blown it. I should have thought ahead, planned this better and booked the tickets. I'm so sorry. We'll never get in now."

"Don't worry, it doesn't matter."

It didn't at all. It was a lovely sunny day and I could think of much better things to do than sit in a dark cinema for two hours (I wasn't sure I would have been allowed in anyway) and immediately the most perfect plan came to mind.

"Joe—I've got a better idea. I know what I would really like to do. Would you mind? Joe, what I'd really like is to get the bus back home and let you meet my parents. I'm sure Dad would drive you back to the pub later," I added, a little impulsively.

We got on the next bus but as we walked down the lane, I suddenly had misgivings about my spontaneous action. Should I have phoned home from a phone box and warn them we were coming? What if Mum had had a relapse and was in no fit state to meet anyone? Was it all going to be a huge embarrassment?

We walked into the kitchen together. Dad was preparing a late lunch and Mum was sitting in her dressing gown at the table reading the paper.

"I've…brought home a friend I'd like you to meet…this is Joe."

He went straight up to Mum and shook her hand.

"Hello Mrs Morrison," he said in his serious voice. "I'm so pleased to meet you. I'm so pleased to hear you're on the mend and I've been thinking about you a lot."

Mum looked up at Joe, held his gaze and smiled. And I could tell she immediately found him utterly charming.

Chapter Twenty-Three
Dog Duty

Catherine Van der Hayde had been very busy preparing for her trip. She had written reminders for herself on slim pieces of card cut out from the back of old cereal boxes.

"Ah Lizzy," she said, as I dutifully turned up after college on the following Wednesday evening and presented myself in her sitting room where she was still sorting out papers.

"Ah Lizzy," she repeated and picked up one of the cards that had L M written at the top.

"Now I think you should take the dog blanket and one tin of food with you, the rest of the tins are in a carrier bag and I'll drop them off tomorrow morning. I won't bother Jennie. I'll just leave them on the doorstep. I've counted sufficient to last until next Friday."

"Are you going anywhere nice, Auntie Cath?"

She ignored my question and continued to study her home-made memo.

"Key," she said consulting her list. "Lizzy, I'm going to show you where I hide the key. But this is for *emergency only,*" (She stressed these words) "It is highly unlikely you will need to go into the house and I am trusting you." At the 'trusting you', she gave me the sort of hard stare normally only reserved for Spoodles.

We went outside to her garden shed (unlocked of course) and on the left shelf high up was a pair of dusty wooden Dutch clogs and in one of those shoes was her door key.

"Bit of a family tradition and I was delighted to spot these clogs in a jumble sale not long ago—that is after you told me I should start locking up. No one else knows about this hiding place. Well," she added rather darkly, "Not these days."

She continued with her list. 'Post' was the last item and we trooped down the garden with Spoodles following obediently behind.

We came to a wooden box-like construction on the gate.

"Would you mind collecting any mail from this box I had to put up and pushing it through the letterbox in my door? The postman has a thing about dogs and I'm not going to change a good system for the sake of ten days. You only need to do it once or twice."

I could see my old friend was not in the mood for chatting and I was keen to walk home with Spoodles and get him settled for the night, so having got the blanket and one lot of dog food I said goodbye. And then I added "Good luck Auntie Cath."

"Hmm," she replied, a little grimly.

I found two old bowls that Mum was saving for her flower pots and filled one with water, then I discovered a large wicker linen basket that had been put out ready for a bonfire and arranged the blanket inside. It was a perfect fit and it wouldn't matter at all if Spoodles chewed some of the woven willow sticks. I gave him a bowl of food and settled him down in the laundry room. My doggy care duties were going to be enjoyable—especially the walks and Spoodles seemed quite content in his temporary holiday quarters.

* * * * * * * * * *

I quickly established a good routine with my new canine friend. I would get up a bit earlier—easy as it was now mid-May and was light from 6 a.m. —and I would walk Spoodles before breakfast; his and mine. When I got back from college, I would go for a longer walk and that would take us up to tea-time (his and mine). Mum was quite happy to let him out at lunchtime, in fact I think she quite enjoyed having him around especially as Dad was back to working longer hours again.

Joe was not at Youth Club that Friday evening, but to my delight Frankie turned up. She was full of the fun she'd had on the previous weekend's Expedition and wanted to tell me all about it.

"We got lost and I fell over and we had to rescue Katie from a bog and Adam was sick on the coach and threw up all over Mr Mitchell's rucksack…"

Of course, I also thought I should tell her my news but somehow I no longer wanted to share something that had become rather private and very personal, so I said nothing and mercifully she didn't ask as I had no intention of telling an untruth to my friend. Instead, I told her about looking after Spoodles and she readily accepted my invitation to accompany me on one of my dog walking routes the next day.

When I got home there was a note on the table:

Joe rang to give you a message that he was working this evening. I have invited him to lunch tomorrow. Thought you would both like that. Gone to bed early, see you in the morning. Mum.

So it was three of us, plus dog, on Saturday morning and it was rather fun. Frankie was in a very happy mood and thought Joe was hilarious as he was so serious and kept checking whatever she said with immense attention to detail. But after a while I realised he was playing along a bit and being extra formal on purpose. Dad had put together a salad lunch and Frankie, assuming she was invited, stayed too so that made five of us around the table and the fact that my two friends were there made it a rather merry gathering.

It seemed a long time ago since we had had guests for lunch (forgetting Joe's impromptu visit the previous week). Mum seemed more comfortable too and Dad was relaxed. Here we were heading towards June and having such a good time. Was this all too good to be true and how long could it last?

Unfortunately, I was about to find out.

Chapter Twenty-Four
Discovery

The following day on Sunday afternoon, I decided to walk Spoodles across the fields to Auntie Cath's house to complete Duty Number Three on my list and put any post through the letterbox as agreed. Fancy being scared of Spoodles, but then I supposed if one were a postman and came across a lot of dogs how would you know which were friendly and which were not, until it was too late?

I was musing on this fact one field away from her home when Spoodles, who had been happily occupied in his own little doggy world, stopped abruptly and sniffed the air. He gave a low growl.

"Come on boy, nothing to worry about—just going to check the mail."

As we approached the cottage, Spoodles became increasingly agitated. At first I thought he was excited to be home but as his barking got louder and more intense I realised with growing dismay he was displaying the same reaction as he had all those weeks ago when the Intruder had been.

There were no letters in the box so I had no cause to go up the garden path, but by now the dog's behaviour had become so distressed that I thought I'd better just peep through the windows to make sure everything was as it should be.

"All right boy, all right. Calm down." But the dog pawed at the back door and whined.

I thought of Auntie Cath's words and they echoed in my mind; *sometimes you have to do the wrong thing for it to be right*.

Without deliberating further I went to the shed and found the key, unlocked the door and went inside.

I knew immediately someone had been in. There was that lingering smell of something rather disgusting and artificial; some horrible smelling perfume or aftershave signifying the presence of a stranger in the house. This time there was no upheaval and the room looked tidier than it had when I collected Spoodles. It was as if someone now knew he had time to methodically go through all the papers. Everything was stacked up in neat piles and the whole room looked far more organised than ever it could have been with Catherine Van der Hayde's filing system—without the elastic bands of course. I stood and took in the scene. There had been no forced entry. Whoever had come knew where the key was kept, unless he had a spare which I thought was highly unlikely. The Intruder had returned and this time he knew he could go through every last piece of paper at leisure to search for…? **What** was he looking for?

I was still and surveyed the setting not knowing at all what to do. Then I remembered the time I had gone upstairs to the bathroom and seen other boxes in the spare room. I wondered if they also contained documents. I ran up the steps and into the room and this time things looked very different. Three boxes had been emptied and there were papers strewn across the floor. The two remaining boxes were untouched and it would appear as if the 'Someone' had been disturbed and left in a hurry unable to finish his task. I felt a shudder—if he knew where the key was kept and he knew that Mrs Van der Hayde was away, when would he be back to complete his mission?

I sat on the bed and thought. It was no use going through the papers. I had no idea what to look for, and there was no point in having a tidy-up as that would alert him/her when he/she returned. Something was hidden in this cottage that someone was determined to find. There was a highly significant piece (or pieces) of paper stashed away—so important that she was away on a mission and the Intruder was back to complete his quest. The two events were linked I was certain.

If I were Auntie Cath, where would I hide a really important document? Not in a box with other papers, I was sure. I glanced across the room and my gaze fell once again on the picture of the lady standing by the aeroplane who seemed to be looking straight at me.

And suddenly, like a rocket firing in my head, I knew where the document was hidden.

I took six steps across the room, lifted the frame off the hook and walked back down the rickety stairs with it tucked under my arm. I locked the kitchen door and Spoodles followed me outside to the garden shed where I replaced the key in the clog.

"Come on boy, back to my place."

Sometimes you have to do the wrong thing for it to be right.

153

I'd had a jumper tied around my waist and as I got nearer home, I took it off and placed the picture inside. It looked just like I was carrying a chunky frame inside a knitted sweater. Nothing else I could do and the one thing on my mind was to get it upstairs to my bedroom without anyone noticing. I went into the laundry room to deposit Spoodles and then I had an idea—I would place the picture under the dog blanket, say 'Hi' and then check the coast was clear. Mum must have thought my behaviour rather odd because, just as I was casually saying hello and chatting about her afternoon, I had a sudden horrible vision of the dog getting into his basket, lying on the picture and breaking the glass.

"Just need to go and check on Spoodles, see you later." And with that I dashed out of the living room.

The picture, still safely in one piece, lay on my bed with the rather unnerving image of Catherine Van der Hayde staring up at me. With shaky hands I turned it over and examined the back of it. There were small neat metal clips holding the back board in place and these easily swivelled so that I could remove it. Then there was a cream-coloured sheet of plain paper and behind that—one blank, unsealed, envelope.

It wasn't one document; it was two. I unfolded each in turn and spread them on the floor then I sat cross-legged on my rug with my arms folded and scrutinised each piece of paper.

The first one: a Marriage Certificate and written in French.

The second one: A three-folded document on much thicker paper, also written in French. I'd seen some of my father's legal documents and knew that this was very important. It had a crest and several signatures but my school-girl French had no hope of translating words like *notwithstanding* and *hereunto*. At best it seemed as if someone was entrusting something to someone else.

I sat lost in thought and conjecture for a long time. Then I remembered I'd told Mum I'd be back in a minute and I must have been half an hour at least. I did not want to arouse her suspicion and I certainly didn't want anyone walking into my bedroom.

I carefully folded the papers and put them in the envelope behind the photograph, replaced the back sheet and the board and swivelled the hinges into place. Then I put the picture into my sports bag with my PE kit wrapped around it protecting the glass. I topped off the whole bundle with a pair of extra sweaty socks—probably the best deterrent I could imagine.

What was I going to do, and who on earth could I ask for help and advice that I could rely on to keep a secret and who also knew about important historical documents?

Chapter Twenty-five

Mr Cook

The big worry for me was that Elsa would want to hang around after our History had lesson finished and nab me to discuss the Sandwich Station idea. How was I going to make it seem that I wasn't trying to avoid her? (I was). And what excuse could I give so that I wouldn't upset her? (Oh, the irony). In the end I wrote a note:

Hi Elsa, I'm really looking forward to planning our fundraising project together but I can't do it this week as I've got rather a lot on and on top of everything else I'm dog-sitting for a friend. So sorry—maybe next week?

I dropped the note on her table as I came in and watched her read it with a concentrated expression, then she glanced up, saw me and gave the 'thumbs up' beaming.

Question: how does one concentrate for a whole double period of History when you have in your possession someone else's stolen property?

Answer: with great difficulty.

"Mr Cook," I hesitated as the lesson ended. "Could I have a word with you?"

"Of course Lizzy."

I was unusually nervous.

"I've got some documents…and an old photograph…they're not mine…I've sort of borrowed them until Friday. And I was wondering if you could have a look…and give me your thoughts?"

"Of course Lizzy."

There was nothing for it. Everyone had left the room and we probably only had a few minutes before someone might come in and disturb us. I took the picture out of my bag and laid it face down on the table so that I could remove the back. I carefully took the two items from the envelope and spread them out and then I turned the picture the right way up so that the photograph of *Haarlem 1939* was also staring straight up at us.

Mr Cook stood completely still and for a whole minute said nothing. Then he made a curious noise in his throat, a bit like a startled exclamation whilst being strangled.

"Lizzy…goodness. Goodness…Lizzy." He appeared to have gone into a distant land and was having a dream. Then he came to his senses and collected his thoughts.

"Lizzy, I have to go and teach the Second Years in a minute. Would you mind, could I possibly take these and look at them later in more detail? I know how special they are and I will take great care, really I will. But my French is a bit inadequate when it comes to legal stuff and translation and I need to do some careful research."

With trembling hands, he folded the papers and slid them shakily into the envelope. Then the board was back in its place with the clips holding it firm.

"I must dash. I'll take good care and keep them safe. Thank you Lizzy. I suggest you keep this quiet for the moment."

I had absolutely no intention of doing anything else.

* * * * * * * * * * *

It was with a certain amount of misgiving that I caught the bus home that evening minus my stolen/borrowed treasure. Mr Cook hadn't been to find me and I didn't know where he would be. I assumed he had been teaching all afternoon and planned to look at the papers that night. But it was troubling me that the picture and its contents were no longer in my possession. How safe was safe? My mind was churning away as I walked home and it was still in overdrive later when I walked Spoodles—in the opposite direction to the cottage.

Where was Auntie Cath and what was she doing? Why didn't she go to the police the first time her unwelcome visitor had turned up? What was the connection between the documents and the photograph (other than a picture frame being a good hiding place) and finally, and most importantly, what did I know about the Life and Times of Catherine Van der Hayde?

The answer to the last question was disturbingly simple: very little. She must have been married as she was a 'Mrs' but that didn't necessarily imply she was still married. Was she divorced and was the intruder her ex-husband? This was a possibility, but surely the divorce courts would have got involved if he was a potential threat and even Auntie Cath would have been sensible enough keep her house locked all the time if she suspected some sort of vindictive repercussions. What about her surname, it certainly was unusual, was she on the run escaping from some far-off land and could it actually be a Private Detective who was entering her property to gather some evidence for a prosecution? I didn't know Auntie Cath very well but one thing was certain to me; a criminal she was not.

And finally, her work as a freelance journalist writing papers and articles and always busy at her desk. Had she turned up some important information about someone else, someone who didn't like her research and wanted to destroy what she had written? But if that was so, where was the connection with such a personal photograph and the papers I had found?

I simply had no idea. I couldn't contact Auntie Cath. I couldn't go to the police and I certainly didn't want to tell anyone else what I'd done, not Joe, not Frankie, not Mum and Dad. There was nothing I could do. I just had to rely on Mr Cook.

I was on tenterhooks all day waiting for our History lesson, the last class on a Tuesday. I had my sports bag ready so that I could bring the picture safely home. Lying awake in the early hours that morning I had arrived at a rational decision; I would take the picture intact to the cottage that evening where I would hang it back in its rightful place. If someone then came and took it before Auntie Cath arrived home on Friday it was just bad luck. I was entrusted look after her dog and definitely not expected to share someone else's private documents with a stranger, even though he was my History Teacher. Mum was still not 'through the woods' and we were waiting every day for news as to whether her operation had 'positive results'. Furthermore, I had exams coming up and a proper boyfriend with whom I was not spending enough time and a fundraising project to sort out with a partnership I wanted to preserve at all costs. There was just too much going on. Why was I worried about a silly picture?

Not surprisingly, the day went far too slowly and I was the first to sit down in our History room. But when the time came for our lesson to begin and in walked Mrs Banks my heart missed a beat and then pounded against my chest.

"Mr Cook's not able to take you today and I have a message for you. Listen carefully. Please read Chapter Ten from your text books and answer the revision questions at the end." She sat down with a pile of marking she'd brought with her and clearly expected the rest of us to settle down in silence too.

My hand went up, "Is Mr Cook not well?"

A sigh: "I don't know."

Pause. My hand again,

"Do you know if he'll be in tomorrow?"

Another sigh and she placed her pen down in exaggerated irritation on the table. "I *don't know.*"

I didn't like Mrs Banks, not many did, and she wasn't renowned for her effective teacher/student communication. Case in point, and everyone else was quiet.

Chapter Ten made utterly no sense to me at all. At that moment, nothing in History made any sense, or indeed in life according to Lizzy May Morrison, and it was with a sinking heart that I got the bus home, my sports bag over my shoulder with socks in it that needed washing.

Wednesday: 08:55. Knocking (a little timidly) at the staff room door:

"Oh sorry to trouble you, I wonder—could I have a word with Mr Cook? If he's available, that is?"

"Not here, sorry."

Why, oh why, did it have to be Mrs Banks opening that door?

I saw Joe briefly but I was grumpy and self-absorbed and I think he must have assumed I was extra worried about Mum. I played in a netball match that afternoon and Miss Russell watched me let two goals go in that I could easily have saved.

"What's up with you Lizzy, mind on other matters?"

(You could say that).

Dog walk with Spoodles when I got home. Should I check the post again? No, I couldn't bear to go near the cottage. Two more days to go.

Thursday: 08.50, Staffroom again (please don't let it be Mrs Banks).

Mrs Paynter, "Oh hello Lizzy, how are you?"

"Er, fine. Just wondering, I have Mr Cook for History and I need to have a word with him. Is he there by any chance?"

"Hang on." (Ray of hope)

"No sorry, no one knows what is the matter. But he can't be that bad, he's sending messages in with work for the cover tutors to read out. Sorry Lizzy, can I help you at all?" (Now that would take some explaining).

Friday morning. Last chance, but I feared the worst and had already guessed the result: *Sorry, but I'm sure he'll be back next week.*

I didn't want to see anybody. I couldn't concentrate and felt utterly exhausted. Not surprising, I hadn't slept for three nights.

There was nothing for it, I had to return Spoodles and I had to face the Wrath of Mrs Catherine Van der Hayde for I was sure she would be extremely angry with me and that would be the end of the happy Auntie Cath/Lizzy May friendship. There was still the option to lie and pretend that someone else taken the picture and I had spent many wakeful moments working on this possibility. Somehow, however, this decision did not square up with my experience of sitting in the church and getting to know Joe more and going to the Youth Club and being so involved with Mum's illness. Implying that it was nothing to do with me was not in-keeping with the 'Re-evaluating Myself Opportunity' and, as fearful as I had become, I was strong and brave enough to tell the truth.

I arrived home and decided I would get this awful event over with as soon as I could. Mum was waiting for me and I thought she was wanting to say something but so preoccupied was I in getting my mission completed and out of the way for good (for I was surely never going to be having cups of coffee in a cosy kitchen again) that I simply said *Hi* and *it's OK isn't it if I take Spoodles back straight away*?

I gathered up the blanket and the last tin of dog food and got Spoodles' lead.

"Come on boy, we're going to take you home." Oh, oh how heavy was my heart.

Mrs Van der Hayde was definitely back for the Land Rover was parked in its normal place and the kitchen door was open. A bicycle was propped up by the garden gate next to her makeshift letterbox, but I gave it little attention.

As I stood at the door, I opened my mouth to speak the lines that I had been rehearsing as I'd plodded through the fields, but they were immediately drowned out by Spoodles' happy woofing.

"Oh wonderful, you're back! Well-done Lizzy. Come in, Come in."

I stepped into the kitchen.

"Auntie Cath," I hesitated. "I've got something to tell you I've…" I glanced into the sitting room and stopped. I couldn't get another word out. I stood and stared at what seemed to be an Apparition calmly drinking a cup of tea and sitting comfortably in one of her chairs. My mouth stayed open, unable to utter a sound.

"Lizzy, come in, come in—come and meet my visitor but I believe the two of you already know each other; this is Brian."

As I entered the sitting room the Ghost got up and came across.

"Lizzy I'm sorry, I'm sure I owe you an apology. You must have been rather worried." (Under-statement). "But it was rather important that I hung on—aha no pun intended—to this artefact because well, I'm sure Catherine will explain that it's thanks to your intelligent action and smart thinking the other day that our relic has survived. But first I'll just go and put this back where it belongs. Now let me see, you said it lives on a hook in the spare bedroom. Am I right? I'm sure I'll find it."

He reached down to the side of the chair in which he had been sitting and picked up the picture—*the picture*—and we heard him walk up the creaky stairs.

"Lizzy May," Auntie Cath came towards me smiling. "I'm sure you've had cause to be very worried, but in fact you've saved…"

Whatever she was about to say by way of an explanation was suddenly caught short by the sound of a car coming to an abrupt halt on the gravel and then a lot of barking. And into the sitting room walked a short dark stranger (he wasn't handsome either). He let out a bit of a kick at Spoodles and ordered "Non!"

Mrs Van der Hayde stiffened. "Hendrick," she announced coldly.

He was just over five feet tall, middle-aged with dark brown hair and he wore a pink shirt, red cord trousers and the horrible smelling aftershave. He glanced around the room, noticed me and dismissed me as if I were just a mere kid and nothing to worry about.

"Hendrick," repeated Auntie Cath, a little louder as if announcing his presence.

"I have come, and what you have belongs to me *Miss* Edwards," his sneering words sounding rather alarming with his strong French accent.

"I think not."

Hendrick looked threatening and I did not like to imagine what might happen next. Perhaps no one in that room, least of all Hendrick, was prepared for what did happen next.

Down to the last two steps came Mr Brian Cook, minus the picture of course. He stood, surveying the scene from his vantage point. A smile played on his lips and he looked poised—like a conductor expectantly waiting for the right moment to lift his baton. He took three strides into the room and stood opposite the unwanted guest as if squaring him up. Then, without a word and quick as a flash, he took a big swing aiming his right fist straight into Hendrick's jaw and knocking him backwards on to the floor.

The impact was astounding.

"Ow, ow, ow!"

"Get up you imbecile," he ordered, "Or I'll kick you where it hurts."

Hendrick still groaning rolled over and my—yes—My History Teacher advanced.

"No, no, no."

"Then go. Get out of here and never come back. Or it will be more than a couple of teeth next time."

I could already see the blood making a scarlet trickle down the pink shirt; it would match the red trousers when it reached them. Hendrick stood up, swaying a little and clutching his face as if holding it together.

"I'm going. I'm going." And he stumbled out.

Brian felt his hand and winced, "Hmm, bit out of practice I'm afraid. But we won't be seeing him again, ever. Gone for good."

Hendrick would not be going to be police. He had entered a place where he was not supposed to be and if the police had taken his fingerprints they would have found hundreds of them all over Mrs Van der Hayde's property and private papers.

Auntie Cath went towards the kitchen, "Another cup of tea, Brian?"

"Maybe not. Probably ought to cycle home and get this thing strapped up."

"Nonsense, you're not going anywhere on that bike. We'll put it in the Land Rover and I'll run you back into town. I owe you a favour."

She turned to me:

"It's been rather a long day—well several long days, but a good outcome in many ways.

"I think," she continued looking hard at me, "It's time to tell you *My Story* all the way through from start to finish, after all you are a part of it now. But it will take a while and Brian doesn't need to hear it again. Would you be able to pop round tomorrow morning and we'll have a cup of coffee—well, several actually?"

It seemed like a good idea. I was exhausted and my head was reeling. I would walk home slowly, give Youth Club a miss, have something to eat and just tumble into bed…

Chapter Twenty-Six

News

Dad was sitting on his own at the kitchen table when I got in.

He looked odd. His right eyelid was drooping and he had a kind of embarrassed grin on his face.

"Lishy!" He exclaimed. "Lishy, you're home. Welcome. Welcome to the party. We're having a bit of a Schellebration…" And with that, he waved a glass tumbler around in an uncoordinated fashion.

I stood in abject horror for the second time that evening and stared at my father. It became apparent that the 'we' was him and a bottle of whiskey.

"Dad," I said, "Where's Mum?"

"Mum, Mummy, Jennie," he giggled, "Darling Jenny is having a bath."

I had never in my life seen my father in this condition.

"Some Good News, let me pour you a glass."

"No thanks Dad."

"Nonsense, girl. Nonsense. Good for you. Puts hairs on your chest."

I was becoming rather proud of my developing 34b Cup and certainly wasn't going to let any chest of mine get ruined with the after-effects of alcohol.

"Just a wee dram, a wee dram," implored my tipsy Dad with such an appalling Scottish accent that I thought if he ever decided to join our local Amateur Dramatic Society I would personally write to the organisers and warn them off him.

He took another swig of the colourless liquid and as he did, I noticed a formal looking letter on the table. Suddenly, I understood.

My Wonderful Father—who for the last six months (probably longer) had lived through the hellish thought that he might lose his wife, and with that his life and all that it meant for him. But my father being the discreet and quiet type had shouldered it all, rarely getting cross, keeping everything going and putting on a brave face. The Office was under control and his clients were happy because somehow, somehow, he'd pulled out all the stops and soldiered on, holding himself together, not even allowing himself to catch my germs when I was so ill.

The moment he'd been dreading and holding himself together against for weeks had now arrived, and he had prepared himself for the worst never daring to believe a wild dream because what would happen if it didn't come true? And now the waiting was over; Good News had arrived, perhaps it wasn't perfect—things rarely are—but there was Hope and it was a cause for celebration.

And My Wonderful Father who rarely drank—we hadn't bought alcohol for months owing to Mum's medication and illness—had found the only bottle in the house; a regular Christmas present from one of the old clients and given to us every year. It would sit at the back of the cupboard gathering dust for seven months and then be donated to the annual Summer Fete for the first prize raffle draw.

But My Wonderful Father, who by some discipline, strength and stoicism beyond all comprehension for so long suddenly had the most compelling need to let go and celebrate the moment he had hardly dared to believe would happen. So he took Neville Barrington's finest Scotch from the shelf and poured himself several generous measures. And then some more.

In spite of everything I laughed. We both did, but at the back of my mind I had a rather alarming vision of having to get my drunken father up the stairs and help him into bed.

Thankfully at that moment Mum came into the room with a towel over her hair. She stood and looked at Dad.

"CHRISTOPHER!" She exclaimed. (She **never** calls him that).

"JENNIFER!" My father replied and giggled, thinking he'd made a very clever retort.

It was enough. I wasn't hungry anymore and my tiredness was overwhelming.

I would leave them to it and go to bed.

Mum's news would be another story I'd have to hear in the morning.

Chapter Twenty-Seven
Story

She was making two cups of coffee as I came into the kitchen,

"Lizzy, good timing. I was going to take a cup up to your father but you might as well have it. I think it will be a while before he wakes up anyway," she gave a wry smile. "Sleep well?"

"Wonderful thank you. I'm sorry I rushed off yesterday with Spoodles without hearing your news."

"Oh don't worry, now is nicer anyway. Let's sit down the two of us and have some breakfast."

"You sit Mum, I'll do it."

We sat quietly while I munched my way through several pieces of toast and then, as we sipped our coffee:

"They will always want to keep an eye on me of course, and I have to go back for an appointment in four weeks but if that goes OK it will be a check-up every six months."

"Oh Mum that's wonderful," I reached across the table and she cupped her hands around mine and I rested my head on top. Then she moved one hand away and stroked my hair.

"It's funny," she said thoughtfully. "There had been something troubling me for many years and while I was so ill I did a lot of thinking…and some letter writing." (She didn't elaborate). "It was as if I had to let something go. Easier said than done of course, but I had a feeling—I don't know, I can't explain it but a few weeks ago I had a feeling I was going to be all right, and five days after the operation when I was able to sit more comfortably I felt—I felt sort of cleansed inside. It seemed as if all the bad bits had been taken away and I was healed from the inside out."

We didn't say much more. A mother and her fifteen-year-old daughter sitting on a Saturday morning at the kitchen table sipping cups of coffee, an ordinary day in late May with all the usual things to do and think about. Except that it wasn't ordinary at all. In our minds the little Morrison family had visited death and wondered what it would be like for each of us in our separate ways; my mother with all her pain; my father with all his responsibilities, and me—goodness Me—with so much activity and different people in my life. But in my quieter moments I had done a lot of thinking. I'd reflected on my special time in the Church—my 'Re-evaluation' as Auntie Cath would have called it—and it seemed to me that doors had opened; doors of forgiveness and doors of acceptance and letting go.

And the things that I had asked for so earnestly had indeed been given unto me.

* * * * * * * * * *

Auntie Cath was also making coffee when I arrived. We took up our normal positions on the stools even though the stove was no longer lit.

"I will start at the beginning and please do say if there is something you don't understand—this may take a long time.

"I was born in 1920. We lived in Sussex near the coast and I was Catherine Edwards, well of course you would know that from my Marriage Certificate."

I blushed but my friend continued unperturbed.

"I don't remember my father, he died when I was two. It was only four years after the war had ended—First World War that is—he had been wounded and never fully recovered. However, he'd been an officer so my mother had a widow's pension and she also worked as a private secretary to an Accountant so we weren't poor and I had a good education. Mother's parents lived in the West Country and every summer the two of us would get on the train and go and visit them for a fortnight. We did it all through my childhood and teenage years and I got to know my Grandparents well and the area they lived in. They had a thatched cottage in a tiny village near Dawlish in South Devon, a few miles from the coast and it was surrounded by farms. Their nearest neighbours were farmers called the Morgan's and Mother and I would help them in the fields when I grew older.

"I suppose I was a rather independent child being the only one and not having a father but a busy working mother (unusual in those days) and I often had to fend for myself finding my own way on buses, trains and such like. It seemed that I was destined to follow in my mother's footsteps and become a secretary, she'd already taught me short-hand and shown me how to type, but it was a journalist that I really wanted to be and when I waited in her office after school I would read the newspapers.

"I was due to finish my education in July 1938, a month before my eighteenth birthday and I knew I needed to do something about getting a job. But I had a wandering spirit and I was desperate to travel and see a bit of the world and it didn't seem to matter to me at all if I had to do it on my own. One late afternoon in June I was reading through Friday's *Times* and an advertisement in the 'Situations Vacant' column caught my eye. It was a French family living in the Netherlands wanting a live-in English nanny to look after their three-year-old son. The bit that really attracted me was the line which said: 'Must be willing to travel.'

"In those days you had to post your application and include two letters of recommendation. My headmistress wrote one and my mother's boss wrote the other one and I suppose it was these references that got me the job. Looking back now I realise how intrepid I was—I was just eighteen but the world was beckoning and I was ready for adventure. My mother wasn't going to stand in my way—we were both very good letter-writers and knew that our regular correspondence would keep us close and well-informed so, armed with my Birth Certificate (which my mother always kept safely for me) I applied for a passport, and it was with her blessing that I left Sussex for Holland that August.

"The family surname was Vormann and they lived in a fashionable part of Haarlem in a large town house over-looking the canal. The husband, who was Dutch, was called Emil and he worked in a bank. Their son was named Matthias (generally referred to as Mattie) and the mother, who was French, was Louise. As soon as I met them, I knew it would all be fine and that Louise and I would get on very well indeed, after all she was only in her late twenties. Mattie was a sweet boy who could already speak Dutch and French but Emil and Louise wanted me to teach him English too.

"It was what you might call 'high society', Louise did a lot of entertaining and there were many friends who dropped by regularly. I discovered that she had a rare and interesting job for a woman; she imported fine wines from France and supplied restaurants in Haarlem and Amsterdam and various well-to-do private businesses and households, so there was always a lot of coming and going and visitors to their home.

"One evening about four weeks after I had arrived Louise told me some friends were coming to dinner and, as I was treated as part of the family, naturally I was invited too.

"I gave Mattie his bath as usual and then read him three stories; one in English, one in French and one in Dutch. My French wasn't too bad but my Dutch was terrible—Mattie would giggle and say, *you got it wrong Cathy-Miss*. (That's what he called me).

"I remember I heard the front door opening and closing and laughter coming up from the floor below and the sound of glasses being chinked together as I said goodnight to him and went downstairs.

"I was just an eighteen-year-old nanny from England wearing ordinary clothes and as I walked into the room with the young Movers and Shakers of the 1930s Netherlands I suppose I could have felt a bit out of place. But Louise was, as ever, engaging and inviting and announced to her guests in French: *This is Catherine Edwards our English au pair and she's very exotic!*

"A man in his mid-twenties looked up and smiled at me and two things happened simultaneously. Firstly, I realised this was the most attractive and intelligent looking man I had ever met and secondly, I felt my heart miss a beat and the blood rush to my cheeks.

"We sat down to eat a rather splendid dinner prepared by Louise. Emil was the wine waiter and served the food. When the meal was over, I got up to help and the handsome guest offered too. We found ourselves together in the kitchen and he (in English with an alluring French accent) said, *So, you are the famous English Nanny. What is exotic?*"

"Of course, I blushed again.

"He told me that he was living and working in nearby Amsterdam as a journalist and reporting mainly on French politics and current affairs for a Dutch newspaper. Just then Louise came into the kitchen with a stack of plates: *Oh Catherine (she exclaimed) I'm sorry I haven't introduced you properly, this is my brother. Meet Paul—Paul Van der Hayde.*

"Before that evening was over, I discovered a few more facts about the family. Louise and Paul were French, of course I realised that; their parents owned a vineyard and lived in the south of France with another son still at home. However there was a Dutch connection, something to do with grandparents— that is how Louise had met Emil **and** it explained why the family name of Van der Hayde was typically Dutch-sounding.

"It was nearly time for the guests to leave but Paul sought me out: *So, the famous English Nanny?* I remember him speaking these words with a broad smile on his face. *How about something really exotic—how would you like to come up and see my aeroplane?*"

Auntie Cath had been speaking for an hour and she paused, got up, stretched and put the kettle on again. I was absolutely entranced.

"Of course it was love at first sight," she continued after settling herself down again with a second cup. "We both felt it and wanted to spend as much time together as we could. There was a little airfield just to the west of town and Paul had a motorbike. Every weekend and any other spare time we had he would come and pick me up. His aeroplane was a Tiger Moth imported from England and it was then four years old. *I was 21 when I got my Pilot's licence,* he told me, *and a year later I blew all my savings on a Moth!*

"But irresponsible, Paul was not. He was kind and clever and immensely capable. He was from a well-to-do family who worked hard and invested wisely.

"It came to my first Christmas and I would have been allowed to go home but I didn't feel the need—besides I was invited with the family, including Paul, to go down to France to spend the New Year with Monsieur and Madame Van der Hayde who were introduced to me as Pierre and Marie.

"We travelled by train through The Netherlands and Belgium and then into France. It was fabulous for me who, until four months ago, had never been further than Devon. The family lived in a small Chateau just outside Saint Emilion deep in the heart of the wine growing region of Bordeaux.

"I was given a lovely welcome and you could say that life was near-perfect; here I was with a wonderful family doing an immensely rewarding job for which I was getting paid, learning a new language and travelling through Europe and, on top of it all, I had a boyfriend with whom I was madly in love. But as ever in life, one has to make allowances, and there were two dark clouds on the horizon.

"The first black cloud was political and going to affect us all in different ways and this was the developing tensions of the time. Our New Year celebrations for the start of 1939 were overshadowed by the goings on in Europe, and Germany in particular. The Van der Hayde's were of Jewish descent although Emil, Louise's husband, was not. I don't know how well you know your history Lizzy, but the annual Nuremberg rallies had been growing in popularity with hundreds of thousands of Germans saluting Hitler and his fascist regime.

"The second dark cloud was specific and aimed directly at me. Louise was twenty-nine, Paul was twenty-six and the younger brother was the same age as me. I don't know whether it was because of that and he saw me as a threat or whether he was just 'wrong in the head' but he took against me straight away. They say that some families have a Black Sheep and he was exactly that. I'd noticed he was often unhappy and the few of his friends I met once or twice were not very pleasant either. I mentioned this as a sort of joke to Louise but she just shrugged it off and said *he's always been like that—so different from Paul and me.*

"Paul wasn't much help either and it just seemed as if the whole family, parents included, tolerated the behaviour of this rude and difficult young man. His name—as I'm sure you will have guessed—was Hendrick."

Spoodles gave a shuffle and she got up to open the door but he just turned around and settled down again. Auntie Cath put down her mug and continued.

"Spring came and things started to hot up with the International scene. We tried hard not to let it worry us. The Vormann family and I were in Haarlem and Paul was still working in Amsterdam and every weekend when the weather was good enough, we would go flying. After a few sessions

Paul let me take the controls and I suppose I started to get quite competent. One day he introduced me to the Instructor who worked at the airfield.

"This is Captain Triggol and he is going to fly with you and teach you properly. Don't worry Cathy, I'm paying for you to have formal flying lessons.

"Paul, being a Journalist, was also a good photographer and had an extremely nice camera. Eventually it was the day of my solo flight.

"Stand by my plane Lizzy and let me take a picture of this moment. I stood and posed rather keen to get going for the first time on my very own in the cockpit and I wasn't too happy about being interrupted.

"Not many weeks later I got my Private Pilot's Licence and we flew together all through the summer of 1939. Then the autumn came and with that, the start of the Second World War.

"I had a letter from Mother telling me she'd sold the house and planned to move out of town and was going to live with my grandmother in Devon where it was a lot safer. (Grandfather sadly had had a heart attack and was no longer alive).

"We knew it was coming of course, Paul being a journalist was privy to a lot of information not normally known by ordinary folk. Louise, also, with her influential contacts and Emil in the banking business; they were all acutely aware of how dangerous the situation was getting across Europe, and the Netherlands in particular.

"We didn't go down to see the family in France that second Christmas but stayed put in Haarlem trying to make it as jolly a time as possible, but when the Spring of 1940 came and the Nazi's invaded Denmark and Norway in early April, we knew it was time to get out.

"One night things got very bad. There were shots in the street. Somebody was dragged out of their house and there was a lot of screaming and shouting and Mattie was terrified.

"In the morning Emil went to the bank but by lunchtime he was home accompanied by Paul. They had heard from reliable sources just how dangerous things were going to get and it was time to make a plan.

"Louise, Mattie and I were to leave by train to travel back to France and stay in the Chateau. We were to head west to Paris and then go south. Paul said he would follow on as soon as he could as he had some important reports to get finished. Emil, too, would stay on in the family house but leave as soon as he was free. We actually left the next day—that was how urgent it was. We packed up special possessions and stowed them away and took mainly our clothes with us. Lizzy, you have to understand for Louise and Paul the Netherlands was going to become a very dangerous place for Jews to live in."

"What about Mattie?" These were the first words I had uttered for a long time.

"Mattie, too. The Jewish line goes down through the female side so it was particularly important for Mattie's sake that his Jewish mother should escape with him.

"It was a terrible journey. Everywhere was panic and chaos. At one point I was separated from Louise because I was travelling with a British passport.

179

"I suppose you could ask why I didn't return to England. I could have done but I was young and adventurous and didn't see the full implications in the danger of what I was doing. I was employed, I loved my job with Mattie and Louise and I certainly didn't want to be separated from Paul for longer than was necessary.

"We eventually made it to the Chateau and were exhausted. The journey had taken us nearly three days and Mattie was developing a fever, but Marie and Pierre were wonderful and gave us our own quarters in part of the old family home where Louise was going to help with what was left of the wine business.

"We knew we were reasonably safe in the south of France but news of developments further north were very worrying and we feared for Paul and Emil.

"It was late April 1940, about two weeks after we had arrived, and I was outside in the fields one afternoon with Mattie and Louise. It was beautiful weather with clear skies and we heard the drone of a light aircraft in the distance. I looked up and when I had spotted the plane I thought it was a Tiger Moth. It came closer and lower and circled overhead and I was sure it was looking for somewhere to land. Suddenly I knew who it was. I leapt about and waved my arms but he couldn't see me of course. The Van der Hayde's farming neighbours had fields bordering the river and these were large flat grassy meadows—perfect for landing a light aircraft. We all ran as fast as we could and arrived as Paul was talking to the neighbour and discussing where the plane could be put out of sight.

"I know it sounds extraordinary but Paul had flown his Tiger Moth half way across Western Europe completely unscathed (of course we were to realise later that he had done it only in the nick of time). He'd had extra fuel cans strapped into the front seat and once he was in France he had found a field to land in and re-fuelled. He had left at first light and landed at three in the afternoon, so his journey including stops had taken him well over eight hours. You won't know this Lizzy, but if you get a head-wind on the nose of a light aircraft it can slow you down considerably and it feels like you are clawing your way through the sky and making very little progress. You see, he was generally heading in a south westerly direction.

"Perhaps it was the developing war which put life and the important things we value into perspective but that evening after we'd all had a bit of a celebratory dinner, Paul proposed to me. I was only nineteen and he was twenty-seven but by then we had known each other for over eighteen months and we were both completely sure. He didn't have a ring with him but he did have a present for me. In the fuselage of a Tiger Moth the bit at the back behind the seats has some storage space. It's like a small locker which you open with clips from the outside. There's enough room for a small bag and maybe one or two odds and ends. And—you've probably guessed what I'm going to say—wrapped up in his clothes was the picture; the one he took of me just before my first solo flight. He said it had kept him going on his epic journey knowing that I was in the Tiger Moth with him!

"If we thought Paul had an intrepid trip it was nothing compared with Emil who turned up just a few days later. He had taken Paul's motorbike which he'd left at the airfield and ridden it all the way through Holland, Belgium and France.

He said it had been the 'Journey from Hell' and all his muscles ached but Louise and I teased him because it had taken him less time than our horrid train ride, **and** he hadn't got covered in fleas—ugh!

"In normal times a wedding of the older son would have been a lavish affair for a family such as the Van der Hayde's, but a war was on which was fast escalating and there was an urgency in all of us that wanted something to celebrate immediately. That is, everyone except Hendrick. So a wedding was hastily arranged with very little planning. We were married in the first week of May 1940 in a small local church and Mattie was a pageboy for me. Not having a father, Emil gave me away as well as being Paul's Best Man.

"Of course, I would have loved my mother to be there but Paul and I were determined to go to Devon as soon as the war was over and have another mini-celebration just for her and my grandmother. We had a three-day honeymoon in a borrowed car in the Loire Valley staying where we could in hotels which were open. When we returned, we were given the keys to a former farm-worker's cottage in the grounds of the Chateau and it was to be our home until peace arrived and we could find somewhere else. I suppose looking back everything was rather rushed but they were different times.

"The Van der Haydes were a well-respected family and—without being too explicit—if you wanted to be intimate with each other you really needed to be married. I'm sure you know what I mean. We couldn't wait any longer."

I believed I saw my old friend blushing as she recalled the memory of those heady days.

"But," she continued. "Paul, being the conscientious and committed type of man that he was, had some important reports to get done for his newspaper in Amsterdam, and Emil also had to get back to the Netherlands. The plan was that Paul would go back and wrap up his job, pack away his few belongings and return the keys to his landlord. He had no reason to be in Amsterdam and his most precious possession was now safely in a make-shift hangar—well, maybe his second most precious possession.

"I reckoned at the most it might be about ten days before I would see Paul again. Louise, too, knew that Emil was planning to do a similar thing although it would take him longer to sort things out. We waved goodbye to them both from Saint Emilion railway station on 8th May 1940. And that was the last time we ever saw our husbands."

I clapped my hand across my mouth and gave a gasp: "NO, Auntie Cath, NO!"

"Two days later, on May 10th 1940, Hitler invaded Holland.

"You know Lizzy, I've often wondered if Paul also had a premonition and that is why he was so insistent on marrying me in such a hurry. After all, he could have decided to wait and leave it until the summer.

"Paul was a Jew and he was a journalist, so he was a doubly-wanted man. He was sensible of course and kept his head down but he continued to get those reports out and someone must have been an informer. They were terrible times and you couldn't trust anyone. Mercifully he was shot—it could have been much worse. And thankfully we got the news from Emil because the waiting and not seeing him and not knowing what had happened to him would have been awful. As for Emil, he stayed on but he had a large empty house and his wife and child were safely away in France so he took in some Jewish refugees. He was careful, but not careful enough and he was shot too. And mercifully too for Louise there were still contacts who were able to get this information to us. Many years later we discovered that it was someone in the Bank who was the double-agent."

We sat for a while not saying anything. Auntie Cath lost in the depths of her memories and me appalled that perfectly ordinary human beings could be so—so criminal—no, so Murderous, to their fellow citizens. She continued:

"The summer of 1940 became a bit of a hot-bed in and around Bordeaux. It was a strategically important harbour and many different nationalities were converging on the town—especially the Spanish. In June, a free zone called the 'Zone Libre' covering much of the south of France was designated and we were just inside it, but the Germans were everywhere and no-where was really safe. They established a prison at Liborne which was only a few miles from the Chateau. I'm sure you've heard of the French Resistance? Well in our area it was a big movement.

"Louise tried to keep the business going as best she could but there were fewer workers and times were hard; she was grieving of course, and had lost her sparkle and energy.

"As for me, something rose up inside me. I was an English-speaking French woman or a French-speaking English woman whichever way you cared to look at it. Once I'd married I no longer had my Nanny duty to do—after all I was officially part of the Van der Hayde family and Mattie now had his grandparents to look after him. I hated the Germans for all I was worth; they had killed my husband and Mattie's father and everyone was suffering. So I made a conscious decision—I would work for the Resistance Movement, *even if it might cost me my life.*

"To start with there were small things to do such as delivering parcels of food to people in hiding, some translation work and coordinating other supplies. I got Paul's motorbike out of the shed, practiced riding it in the fields and soon I felt I could handle it on the road. Quite honestly, wearing a hat of some description and a jacket and trousers on you couldn't tell if I was a male or female. I became more and more confident at breaking the law and working for the Resistance and continued to perform under-cover operations throughout the rest of 1940 and into the following year.

"Then things got a lot more intense and some important papers needed to be delivered to a Commune 40 miles away and that particular route was too dangerous by road. Someone needed to go across country but that would involve a difficult river crossing. I thought of the Tiger Moth sitting in the neighbour's barn. She hadn't been flown for over a year and I was also out of practice but I was sure it was a possibility. I borrowed Jacques who worked for the family and who was handy with engines and machinery and together we gave the engine a service taking out all eight plugs and cleaning them, doing an oil change and generally checking everything was in order.

"It was a Gipsy Major engine with four cylinders and quite easy to work on. I explained to Jacques how to be The Starter which means that you have to hand-swing the propeller to get the engine going and it can be very dangerous if you don't know what you are doing. That evening Jacques got hold of some paint and a paintbrush and painted out the Moth's registration. This was highly illegal of course as she was now a completely un-identifiable aircraft with no markings. Jacques said it would take a few moments of indecision while the enemy decided if it was friend or foe and that might give me enough time to avoid being shot. Looking back, I think that was rather fanciful because a Tiger Moth is a jolly unique and conspicuous British aircraft, and goodness knows what damage that old paint must have done to the fabric covering.

"I took off the next morning and it was only a short flight. The weather was lovely and it was peaceful below me—it was as if there wasn't a war on at all and it was wonderful to be in the air again. I found the location easily because an unusual windmill marked the spot. I didn't have to land, I just had to drop the bag with its precious contents out of the cockpit getting as close to the windmill as I could.

"I was to do one more mission of a similar nature and then things got extremely challenging. I was asked to fly a wounded Dutch Airman to a destination further up in France. It would be a hugely risky operation as I would be flying only a few miles away from the beginning of the North German Occupied Zone—this was an artificial border the Germans had established in the upper part of France. I was given the most basic of information; the Airman would be brought to the Tiger Moth in the night and we would leave at first light to a secret destination. I would land, deliver my 'goods' and be provided with enough fuel for the return journey. I would be given a map and the compass bearings and a written description of what to look for. Then I was to fly back on my own.

"I thought about the parachute that one should wear when flying longer distances at higher altitudes and made my way to the barn where the plane was stored. I remember Paul had dumped it on a hay bale when he saw me rushing towards him. But when I found it, to my horror I saw that mice had attacked the canvas covering and bits of the silk had been chewed up leaving lots of black droppings and fluffy bits on the hay. There was no way I could get a replacement—I would just have to be extra careful.

"When I awoke on the morning of the intended operation it was obvious there would be no flying that day. The weather had closed in and the cloud was 'on the deck'. That's a flying term which means you won't see where you're going! I went to find Louise and Mattie and have a coffee with her. The wine business was almost non-existent but there was still a lot to do elsewhere. Louise said that her father had asked us all— that is her, Hendrick and me, to his study at 2 p.m. It sounded rather formal and it was. Marie was there too. Pierre was extremely serious; he told all four adults he was worried about the Chateau, the developments in the area and his health. Not knowing how the future would unfold he had come to a decision about his property and he had drawn up a document which was known as a *Promesse de Porte-fort*. It's a very unusual term but basically it's a contract by which a person makes commitments to his or her beneficiaries. He'd had copies made for us and each was dated and stamped with the Chateau's wine emblem and supported with his signature and a Witness. Well, you've seen it, haven't you?" I nodded, (so now I knew).

"I was part of the family he told me, and therefore I was entitled to a one-third share. Marie being his wife was the immediate beneficiary if he died, but upon her death the

Estate (or what was left of it) would be divided between the three of us. Mattie being the only grandson would inherit in due course from his mother who would for the moment act as the Executor. I was astonished to be treated in this way but Pierre was a forward-thinking gentleman and treated everyone fairly and had there not been a war on and Paul had lived it would be years before I might have expected to be included like this.

"The documents were given to each of us and Pierre emphasised the fact that we should look after them with the utmost care. In due time, he said he would draw up a proper Will but for the moment this would suffice. As we left and said goodbye, Hendrick gave me a most peculiar look.

"I put the document in my pocket and returned to my cottage but when I got there Jacques was waiting anxiously for me. He was standing outside smoking and looking agitated and as soon as he saw me he stubbed out his cigarette and ground it into the path with his boot. He said that someone had reported that the English lady at the Chateau might be working for the Resistance and my life was in potential danger.

"*They will come and question you very soon,* he explained, *so you need to be away whilst we provide a safe alibi and remove any suspicion.* I was told to leave everything as normal only bringing a small bag if necessary and I would be taken to a safe place for the night. I had to leave the cottage as it was and give no indication that I wouldn't be returning— my passport for example—must be left in a drawer where it could be obviously noticed. *You must hurry* said Jacques *and I will return with the truck in ten minutes.* I stood and looked around me appalled that someone had blown my cover, then I went into action.

"I put a spare jumper and underwear in a canvas bag I used for going to the market. I left my toothbrush. I left other clothes out on a chair. It was while I was looking for my passport in a drawer to leave it as instructed as a decoy that I noticed my marriage certificate. Something told me that I didn't want a Nazi sympathiser handling this so I put that in my pocket too. Then, just as I was about to leave I saw my picture—my photograph—hanging in the hall. What should I do about that? Evidence of a female pilot was too obvious to give away and they would search and find the aeroplane soon enough. I didn't know where to hide it and time was running out so I took it down and fitted it in the canvas bag.

"I locked the door and put the key in a wooden clog by the doormat and the minute I had done so Jacques pulled up with the truck at great speed. He drove me to another farmer's cottage not far from where the aircraft was kept. I would be safe there for the night he assured me and he would return at 5:30 the next morning. Then he gave me all the papers I needed and hurried away.

"The farm workers were an elderly couple and were terrified and hardly said anything. But they gave me some soup and tea and showed me to a mattress in the attic and I just had enough light to study all the instructions.

"I was up and ready for Jacques to drive me to the makeshift hanger—it took only a few minutes. The Airman was called Joseph and he was in pretty bad shape (scruffy and unclean) but he was probably exhausted and mentally drained from the trauma of his narrow escape more than the ankle injury he had sustained. Jacques and I got the Tiger Moth out and her coverings off, it was a poor attempt at camouflage but something was better than nothing. Thankfully I always stowed my flying things in the plane—that is my leather flying jacket, helmet and goggles and gloves—so they were ready to put on and Jacques had seen there was enough fuel for the flight.

"We got Joseph into the front seat with difficulty and I wondered how I was going to get him out. Then, having checked everything was A-OK around and in the aeroplane I put my bag in the locker, climbed aboard and got strapped in. '*Fuel On, Throttle Set, Contact,*' I stated in order to report the correct starting procedure giving the standard thumbs-up sign with my left hand. Jacques swung the propeller and she leapt into life on the first pull. I did the engine checks and waited for the oil pressure to rise sufficiently on the indicators. Then Jacques pulled away the chocks and I taxied across to a far corner of the field and turned the Tiger Moth into wind.

"We bounced along the grass for less than fifty yards and then I pulled back gently on the stick and we were airborne. I could go into detail about the flight as there were one or two worrying moments but the weather was good and Joseph knew the terrain and where we were heading and helped me navigate by the use of hand signals. We touched down in the appointed field and two men who 'just happened' to be mending a gate came towards us—friends not foes of course. They helped Joseph to get out and at that moment signalled to another pickup truck coming through the field with several jerry cans of fuel in the back.

"But if I thought I had just accomplished the most challenging mission of my life I was mistaken. The driver of the truck approached me: *You are Catherine Van der Hayde, are you not?* He said. *We've had some important news—it's not safe for you to return. Your home has been ransacked and you are a wanted woman. You will be putting your family's lives in great danger if you return. Whatever happens, you must **not** go back.*

"It was still only nine in the morning. It was reasonably good weather and I had an aeroplane full of fuel but I couldn't go back. What was I to do and where could I go? I knew I really only had one option—crazy and dangerous as it sounds—I would fly the Tiger Moth home to England."

Chapter Twenty-Eight
Escape

Auntie Cath got up from her stool and immediately Spoodles jumped up too.

"Dog needs a pee." Glance at the clock: 12:45.

"Goodness, it's nearly lunchtime and I haven't got to the important bit yet. Why don't you stay for a bite? Maybe you should phone home—speaking of which please tell me about Jennie while we have lunch."

I went into the sitting room and made the call. Auntie Cath was underselling her story, fancy not implying it wasn't important so far? But I supposed everything is relative.

Thirty minutes later we took up our positions again.

"In the Tiger Moth there was a small bundle of papers belonging to Paul which contained details about the aircraft and her log-books, and in amongst the items I found old aeronautical maps of Southern England which he had used when he flew the aircraft to the Netherlands from the factory in North London. I decided the only sensible option would be to try and make it to south-west England where I hoped the skies might be quieter and safer than Portsmouth, Southampton and along the Sussex and Kent coasts.

"Eventually I would find my mother, perhaps by train or maybe a lift with someone. I plotted a route as direct as I could which was pretty much due north and a compromise from going too far west and an even greater distance over the sea. Apart from the obvious enemy below me on the ground and around me in the air, the big risk was the immense amount of water I had to fly over. You only have one engine and if that fails you've had it. I certainly didn't want to drown and the stretch of water was going to be a great deal further than a quick hop over the Channel further across to the east. I knew from my newspaper reading days there was a clutch of three airfields in close proximity to each other not too far up from the coast on the Somerset/Dorset border and I thought the chances of finding one of those would surely be better if there were several to choose from! I really didn't know what I would do when I landed, maybe I was thinking I could donate the aircraft to the war effort as Tigers were still being used as trainers for would-be pilots and then I guessed I would try to make my way to my grandmother's cottage.

"I gave the aircraft a good check while the men were putting in the fuel. I had some water to drink and that was it, all I wanted to do was get going and fly to safety.

"Lizzy May—I have to tell you there are moments in life that you sometimes do something so crazy and so risky it is almost as if you are destined to succeed. Here was I, an inexperienced low-hours pilot about to fly an unmarked aircraft in Enemy Territory. In those days there were no clever navigation aids in a small aircraft and Paul hadn't even bothered to get a radio fitted. All I had was a map, a compass and a watch. And once you've studied your map on the ground that's it—any loose bits of paper will blow straight out of the cockpit or into your face when you are in the air. But strange as it may sound the greatest enemy for the pilot even in war-time is always the weather. I had no forecast for the journey and no way of knowing what the cloud base and wind direction would be fifty or so miles further along.

"I took off and as I headed north there seemed to be some small low fluffy clouds gathering below me. At first they were what you might term as 'broken at 500 feet' in aviation language, but within a few miles they became thicker and before I knew it a dense blanket of cloud had formed below me. I was absolutely terrified as I could no longer see the ground and could only guess where I was. I stuck to my Heading and climbed in the bright blue sky above and beyond me. Of course I now realise that this blanket of cloud is what saved me being spotted from the ground and shot at.

"The maximum ceiling height for a Tiger Moth is technically 12–14000 feet but by the time I had reached less than half that height I'd had enough of going up. I was getting extremely cold and I felt I was putting too much strain on the engine and using too much fuel. I levelled off and was cruising at nearly 90 mph. I kept checking all the dials and looking out through the two crossed sets of wires in front of me. There was quite a lot of vibration coming through the left rudder but I knew that was nothing to worry about, and the engine droned on nicely. I also seemed to have a bit of a tail wind which helped and then, in the far distance, I noticed a different shade on the horizon. It was the blue of the coast coming up and I would soon be reaching the start of the English Channel.

"Suddenly, to my absolute horror, out to the north-west I saw a large aircraft—big enough for a Bomber—stooging around probably a bit lower than me. To this day I do not know why he didn't spot me. The only explanation I can think is because of the position of the sun; it would have been about 10.30 in the morning and looking south east is difficult when the sun is shining brightly into your eyes. Objects in the sky, or anywhere for that matter, are far easier to notice when you have the sun behind you.

"For a long time after that I was terribly worried and wondered if he might come up from behind. Below me the clouds were thinning and looking down through the breaks suddenly there I was over the sea and still heading north. The water seemed endless, the drone of the engine and nothing but misty blue all around me. I kept checking my watch and the compass and despite it being the summer I was getting colder and colder. I had hardly slept and I was also extremely hungry. The wind seemed to have changed direction too becoming more easterly than southerly. Visibility was very poor and the haze was getting worse.

"I kept squinting ahead through the wires and, after what seemed like an eternity of the sea below, I eventually thought I could see a speck of land ahead of me and my spirits rose a little—was I going to make it after all? I thought I was on course for that cluster of airfields but as I drew closer to the coastline nothing looked right. Where on earth was I? The Isle of Wight should have been noticeable way out to the north-east but I now know that I had been blown too far across to the west. Never having flown in England I didn't know the lie of the land but I had been good at Geography and thought I knew the positions of most of the seaside towns and the contours of the south coast, but I simply didn't have a clue as to where I was.

"And then, out of the blue, just as I was sure I would finally get clear of the wretched water I heard a noise that every pilot dreads—the engine gave a little cough. At first I wasn't sure if I had imagined it but a few minutes later I heard it again, just as if it were missing a beat. I was at about 6000 feet and in a Tiger Moth you can glide without power for several miles if you set the attitude properly. Suddenly the engine gave a huge splutter and streaks of oil came flying into my face and into the cockpit. Then the engine stopped and everything went eerily quiet. I looked down and nowhere made sense.

"There were some enormous hills to the left and another range of hills way beyond to the north. And directly in front of me was a large estuary. Where was I and where could I land? I was close to blind panic. This was the end I was sure.

"Then I spotted something that hardly registered at first but seemed vaguely familiar—far below was a railway line running east-west and then turning in an acute southerly direction. In a flash I believed that was the main line to the West Country I went on as a child. I swung the Tiger Moth to the left and prayed to the God of Heaven to keep me safe—*please let me find somewhere to land, **please**!* We kept coming down and the closer we got to land the more recognisable the features started to become; the town on the coast to the right of the estuary must be Exmouth and those to the left on the railway line would be Dawlish and Teignmouth and then I knew—miracle of miracles—I was near that old village.

"Somewhere, somewhere, down below was the Morgan's farm with its flat grassy meadows. Down and down we came and every bit of my body was on red alert. If I crashed would the plane catch fire? What was the wind direction and where were the telegraph lines—sometimes they are so hard to spot until it's too late. Three thousand feet…two thousand feet and dropping like a stone. One thousand feet and I was guessing the height anyway because I didn't know the terrain below and the altimeter would certainly have become less accurate owing to the pressure changes in the weather. Eight hundred feet, no time to lose—there was a field in front of me, quickly I unlocked the slot lever, everything too fast and I couldn't slow down. Two hundred feet, one hundred feet and I seemed to be skimming the hedges. Fifty feet, forty, twenty and then the most awful bang as I hit the ground—or rather it seemed as if the ground had risen up to hit me. We were going too fast, I couldn't steady the Tiger Moth and she weaved alarmingly and dangerously from side to side.

"Then I did what is called a Ground Loop of 180 degrees. The aircraft's tail swung too sharply to the left so that we did a half circle and the right-wings tipped and smashed in the ground bringing everything to an abrupt and ungainly halt. Without thinking I had adopted the brace position with my left arm and I had been jolted around but survived. The ground loop actually saved us for at that speed we would certainly have ploughed through the hedge in to the next field which was an old apple orchard. I was shaking and bruised and despite being cold the sweat was pouring off me, but actually I was in much better shape than the poor aeroplane.

"I undid my harness with my slippery fingers and climbed out gingerly shaking all over and just wanting to lie down on the grass—oh the wonderful firm ground—but my interesting arrival had been spotted by Mr Morgan who was coming towards me trundling across his field on an old tractor wondering who had the temerity to land an aircraft in his precious hay meadow. He didn't recognise me of course and was completely astonished, but that's nothing compared with my mother and grandmother when I eventually walked in to the cottage—it would have been the biggest shock of their lives but I won't dwell on their reactions; I'm sure you can imagine their surprise.

"Much later that day while it was still light and I had been plied with cups of tea and hot food we towed the rather sorry aeroplane into an old barn and covered her with sacks and put straw bales in front. The right wings were badly damaged and the tail skid had all but been ripped off but the fuselage and the left pair of wings were in surprisingly good shape. Being made mainly of wood and cotton I think some of the broken bits went on a bonfire. To my absolute amazement the locker was intact so I retrieved my canvas bag and, even more surprisingly, found that the picture had survived including the glass frame.

"So that is the extraordinary tale of how I made it back to England. The Tiger Moth stayed in the barn and I spent the rest of the war with my mother and grandmother in Devon and earned my keep by helping the Morgan's on their farm."

"What happened to Louise, Mattie and everyone at the Chateau?" I asked.

"I wrote to them immediately to tell them I was safe and give them my address. I had to be careful because the post was censored and eventually one of my letters must have got through but it was nearly a year before I had a reply. It was not good news; later in 1942 the whole of France was taken by the Nazi's. Pierre had had a stroke and was not expected to live much longer. Marie was looking after him and Louise was doing what she could to keep the household together. You know, I used to wonder if my actions had caused his stroke—after all it's not every day that a cottage on your estate is ransacked and your only daughter-in-law goes missing. But after a while I decided that he probably had known what I was doing and he would have approved. He was very much like Paul and I was fond of my father-in-law.

"As for Hendrick, apparently there was a bit of a mystery and he disappeared for a while, and to this day I am not entirely sure of things—was he already hunting for my documents to destroy my identity? Did he find my passport and then search for my marriage certificate? It seemed that someone knew where the key was kept to the cottage. It's an awful thought Lizzy, but I did wonder who was The Informer and **who** really did not want me in that family?

"When the war ended, I thought I would go and visit Marie, Louise and Mattie but somehow I never got round to it. Money was tight too. I did go into journalism in a way but it was mainly working from home and I didn't earn much. I corresponded with Louise throughout the 1950s and early 60s and then our letters tailed off to just Christmas and birthdays. After a few years my grandmother died and then my own mother became unwell and looking after her took up a lot of my time. When she died in 1964, I sold the cottage, moved away and bought this place. I just got into a sort of routine here—my past was behind me and I worked hard at writing articles and doing research for people that wanted it. And the little bit I earned kept me in coffee and the old car on the road.

"Then out of the blue four—well perhaps five—things happened and although I didn't realise it at the time they were all connected.

"The first was that I read a piece in our local newspaper by a Historian doing research work for his thesis and needing personal stories of heroism and escape from the war and as you will have guessed, it was Brian Cook. I don't consider myself a hero at all but I thought he might be interested in some of my work for the Resistance Movement. We met up on quite a few occasions at the Arts Centre in Hillerton and I told him a number of things. He was terribly interested and enthusiastic but at the time I didn't give him the full story although now of course he does have the whole account. But I suppose the experience of meeting him and recounting those early war memories had a bit of an impact and perhaps psychologically, I **was** willing to pick up the pieces again.

"Then I had a letter from Mattie—yes, Mattie—not Louise, who by now was in his thirties and he told me that his grandmother Marie was very frail and living in a private care home no longer able to manage her own affairs. And sadly, very sadly, his mother had been diagnosed with an incurable cancer and didn't have long to live." (At this I visibly winced, the legacy of fear was still lurking in my mind).

"Louise had given him Power of Attorney. I'm sure being a Solicitor's daughter you know what that means.

"Mattie explained that his uncle was wanting to sell up the old chateau. I'm guessing that Hendrick knew it would not be long before it was just him and his nephew about to inherit. However, Mattie wanted to honour the wishes of his late grandfather and thought it would be a good idea if I came to France to have a meeting.

"You know Lizzy, here I was in my own home at last with my dog and my bit of work and other odds and ends and I wasn't going to bother with an old promise that had been made in the heat of terrible excitement and tragedy to an English girl of twenty years old.

"But then two other events occurred to make me change my mind. The first you know about; the reappearance of Hendrick. I knew it was him although I couldn't prove it. He always hated me and he hugely resented the fact that I'd been included in his father's will except, of course, it wasn't a Will. It was barely a legal document and if he could find my bit of paper and my marriage certificate and destroy all the evidence that I had in my possession, then the truth of what I was entitled to would no longer be available. He would be able to have my share.

"The church we were married in was bombed and all their records destroyed so it would have been pretty much impossible for me to demonstrate that I was the daughter-in-law of a Chateau Owner in Southern France once Marie and Louise were dead. Mattie was only just five when I left and a child at that age would not be expected to now testify to a fifty-something-year-old woman.

"About the same time as Hendrick's unwanted intrusion I had another letter, this time from the old farm in Devon. Mr Morgan Senior had passed away and his son was now running the farm, and Mr Morgan Junior said what did I intend to do with the heap of junk that was once an aeroplane and taking up space in his late father's barn?

"So I got around to thinking about everything. I knew that Chateau had fallen into disrepair and it wasn't worth a fortune, but if I really was entitled to a one-third share of the proceedings I could spend some money on getting this place tidied up and a new Land Rover—I suppose you could say that is also a bit of a wreck. But what I would love to do more than anything would be to retrieve that old Tiger Moth from the barn and pay to get her rebuilt and re-covered with a new engine fitted and put back in the air. Maybe I could donate her to a flying school? It would give me so much joy and pleasure to see the old plane in use again—that Tiger Moth to which I owe my life. So I made a decision. I wrote to Mattie and said I would come and visit him, and although I was dreading a showdown, I thought *why should horrible Hendrick have what I was entitled to, **even** after all these years?*

"We actually had a lovely reunion. I went to see Marie who is completely with-it even though she is so elderly and frail. And I saw Louise too which was very sad and very difficult, but I'm glad I did it I as we needed to talk and relive our losses all those years ago and I think I did it just in time. Then a Solicitor came to visit us who had been working very hard to get all the business in order. The Chateau will be cleaned out and put on the market in the autumn. Mattie is now the appointed Executor and is seeing to everything, he has grown up into a wonderful and highly respected young man.

"Of course there was one person at our meeting who should have been there but wasn't; one person who knew I was out of the country and at long last here was his golden opportunity to get hold of the evidence and destroy it so that he could have a *half* share and write my name out of the family for good."

She stopped talking and I ran mentally through all the strands that were that were at last coming together. But there were a few unanswered questions.

"Your two documents," I queried, "Surely you needed to take those with you?"

"Yes, I suppose I should have done but I couldn't bring myself to transport those precious pieces of paper all the way back to the south of France. I thought they would be safer here. I'd been lucky with them once and I didn't want to risk it a second time. The Lawyer told me as soon as I got home, I was to go straight to my Solicitors and get what is called a Certified Copy made from each of them and sent through from their office to his. Thankfully that is now in hand. Without a doubt Hendrick was getting very close. He would have eventually found the documents. After all, he'd gone through every box."

"All of them, Auntie Cath?"

"Oh yes, every last one."

(*Ah*).

"So it's thanks to your intelligent thinking, as Brian said last night, that you saved the day.

"By the way, talking of him, did you see that amazing swing he took at Hendrick last night? I was laughing all the way home. Fancy our 'Dr Cook-to-be' was once an amateur boxer? Him, of all people—an Academic!"

We sat in the room, quiet now with the clock ticking in the background and both absorbed in thought. My wonderful friend who had now told me her story and I felt privileged to have heard it. Would I ever share it with anyone? Possibly. When the time was right.

I got up to go, it was midway through the afternoon and then I had a thought; "You mentioned five things Auntie Cath, what was the fifth that happened?"

"Oh that," she replied with a quiet laugh, and for once she looked away and gazed distantly away out of the window.

"A young girl called Lizzy May and a certain woman in her 50s fell into each other's lives."

Chapter Twenty-Nine
Fund Raising

It was now the last week of college before the May holiday and then we would have exams, but I did have two things to look forward to after they were over; one was the History trip to London and the other was my birthday at the end of June. Meanwhile, Elsa and I had to get very busy with our Sandwich Station idea which we decided we would launch the week after the half term break.

We sat down together straight after Monday morning's History lesson.

"I think we should do some posters to advertise it," I said. When I wasn't going over Auntie Cath's story in detail in my mind for about the twentieth time I'd given our project some thought and had already decided the artwork and wording in my head.

"Great idea," replied Elsa. "And somebody mentioned something about having to get permission."

We didn't know exactly what form the permission had to take so Elsa went off to the staff room to ask, and I offered (sounding braver than I felt) to go to the Principal's Office and check.

Meeting up later at lunchtime Elsa was red in the face and exasperated,

"This is hopeless—no one knows anything in this place and I kept getting fobbed off from one person to the next and I'm still not sure what we need to have to prove we can do it!"

I hadn't had much joy either. I'd had an extremely blank and disinterested response from the Principal's Secretary. In the end she had mentioned something about '*Seeing the Caretaker*'.

"OK then, let's go and find Isaac."

He was in the boiler room 'cleaning out the pipes' as he put it, and when he saw the two of us together, he beamed an extraordinarily large smile so that the whole of his face wrinkled up with joy.

"Isaac," said Elsa importantly and coming straight to the point. "Lizzy and I are fundraising for our History trip and planning to make and sell sandwiches in the foyer at lunchtime starting on the first day we get back after half term. Is that all right with you?"

Isaac seemed to find the question highly amusing and gave a deep laugh. "Is that OK with me? Well, maybe I'd have to go away…and consult…myself. But, seeing as it's you two, how many tables do you want me to put out?"

* * * * * * * * * *

After all the excitement and upheaval and goings on from the previous days (and weeks/months), it was good to settle down and concentrate on revision. I saw Joe at college and at Youth Club and when he was free the following week he got the bus to my house. I met up with Frankie as well on some evenings during the half term break. She was also busy with her school work and seemed to have developed a greater sense of dedication to her studies. Meanwhile I had a few days left with Elsa before we broke up for the holiday as we prepared posters and decided on exactly how we would run our event beginning on the first Monday back after the holiday.

* * * * * * * * * *

In the end it was a far bigger and better success than either of us could possibly have imagined. Perhaps it was something to do with the timing because, during the fortnight of exams, our timetables were collapsed and students and staff wanted to eat quickly and at different times. We would start setting up at 11 o' clock and opened from 11:30 to 2:00 pm every day. Whenever I had an exam, I got Carol to help and when Elsa had one she got James to cover. Joe turned up when he could, often at packing up time and was really helpful. In fact quite a few of the others in the History group also pitched in and gave their support.

In the mornings Elsa and I would do any food shopping that was necessary. We had decided to keep our menu simple and opted for sliced bread and a choice of easily assembled fillings: cheese (with or without pickle), ham (with or without mustard) chocolate spread, jam and Marmite. Isaac negotiated some space in the kitchen and a free shelf in the fridge for us to leave stuff overnight. We bought paper plates, paper napkins and plastic cups for the orange and lemon squash and took it in turns for one of us to make the sandwiches and serve, and the other to take the money.

Talking of cash we raised a huge amount—more than everyone else in the group put together and we were considered something as super stars of the show. On the final day of our venture, Mr Green, the Principal (call me Damien) came by and bought a *cheese-no-pickle* sandwich and a plastic cup of lemon squash. He had heard about our enterprise and organised for a Reporter from the *Hillerton Herald* to turn up and produce a short piece on our event. "Good publicity for the college, well done girls! I hear it was your idea Lizzy," he said and he looked directly at Elsa.

A photograph was taken of us standing behind the tables wearing our aprons and the poster advertising *Choose Your Filling* behind us. Then we gave a short interview about our Sandwich Station idea and what we were raising the money for. The young reporter went away but he must have been new at his job and rather keen to make an impression, for when the article eventually appeared in the first week of July the heading in the paper ran:

Runaway Success — Young Girls Raise Lunch Station Cash!

I thought back to a—not entirely dissimilar—heading written in that paper nearly fourteen years ago and decided not to mention anything to Elsa.

Chapter Thirty
The Trip

Exams were over, it was late June and time for the long-awaited History trip.

Mr Cook had been getting efficient, excited and anxious all at the same time and as we were a mixed group, a female member of staff had to accompany us. When I heard it was to be Miss Russell I knew we would all have a good time.

We were to travel up to London by coach in the afternoon and stay overnight at a budget hotel, go to the exhibition the next day and then return home in the evening. I suppose we had all assumed it was going to be the British Museum we would be visiting with all its hundreds of rooms and historical exhibits. But to our surprise, we were going to the National Museum of War as there was a temporary exhibition that Mr Cook particularly wanted us all to see.

We'd had a fun evening all going out together to the Wimpy at Oxford Circus and staying up chatting till the early hours, then we travelled by tube to the Museum and queued to get in and Mr Cook seemed so nervous I wondered what on earth was the matter.

We looked around the permanent exhibitions which were many and varied and on the terrible themes of War but they held our interest and we learnt a lot. Then we went upstairs and Mr Cook was nearly tripping up every step in his excitement. We came to a notice which announced:

'Temporary Exhibition June—September 1972: Unknown Tales of Heroism and Escape of the Second World War.'

It was fascinating; stories and memorabilia about the Nazi occupation and the horrors that people endured. But there were many tales of heroism and big and small acts of kindness and the good news of humanity trying to help each other. We rounded a corner and then I stopped dead and I put my hand to my mouth and gave a gasp. There in front of me, in a huge floor-to-ceiling poster, was a beautifully blown-up reproduction of Auntie Cath's photograph. The enlargement had created an even greater sense of atmosphere; the young woman standing tall and resolute with the browns and creams of the Tiger Moth beside her. I stood still for some moments quietly taking it all in, knowing I would never forget this extraordinary experience.

There were detailed written descriptions as well all about her activities and missions for the French Resistance, this being the result of the meetings held at the Arts Centre. Mr Cook was studying me: "I hope it explains things Lizzy, I only had a short window to get this photograph copied and all my notes typed up for the Exhibition. I couldn't bear to let it out of my sight once you'd shown me. It's the perfect addition to her stories and everyone thinks it's wonderful."

So that's where Mr Cook disappeared for those four dreadful days last month when I was practically killing myself with worry. And when I turned up at her home full of apology and found him having a cup of tea in her sitting room, he had been calmly discussing the forthcoming exhibition with Catherine Van der Hayde.

Of course I had to forgive him, it's not every day you go up to London and read script written by your teacher and see one of your most amazing and wonderfully inspiring friends in a life-size portrait in front of your eyes.

"It's fine," I said. "I understand."

* * * * * * * * * * *

Everyone had drifted off with Miss Russell and it was only my teacher and I still left in the Exhibition. Then, the Curator came up and Mr Cook introduced me to him as *the one who was responsible for lending us the picture.* The Curator, who was short and bald and wore large round spectacles nearly as big as his face, beamed at me. He shook my hand and said how wonderful it all was and then he grabbed Mr Cook's right hand and shook that vigorously too. And I saw my teacher wince.

We walked back down the steps to find the others and Mr Cook said, "By the way Lizzy, I did honour one part of the agreement."

He put his somewhat tender hand into the inner pocket of his jacket and drew out a typed sheet of paper.

"I got a translation done of Catherine's so-called Will, although I wasn't able to replicate the crest and the signatures. Maybe you can keep it somewhere safe!"

Monsieur and Madame Van der Hayde
Château Hayde de la Dordogne
Saint-Emilion
France
10 June 1941

Promise to Person

I, Pierre Van der Hayde, do solemnly declare on this day 10 June 1941 that upon my death I leave the property of Chateau Hayde de la Dordogne and all personal chattels to my wife, Marie Van der Hayde for as long as she lives or so wishes to disperse of said possessions.

Upon the death of Marie Van der Hayde (or earlier if she so wishes) I declare that the sum total of all property and chattels is valued and thus divided in three equal shares to the Beneficiaries whose names are written below. Furthermore, I entrust my eldest daughter Louise Vormann as my sole executor and upon her death, my grandson Matthias Vormann.

Notwithstanding the above declaration a Beneficiary is at liberty to buy out another's share (upon their agreement) if it becomes expedient to retain said property.

IN WITNESS whereof the parties hereto have here unto set their hands the day and year first above written.

Chapter Thirty-One
Gifts

It was the end of June and my sixteenth birthday. Being such a significant time in particular this year for the Morrison family, my parents had decided the three of us would go out to dinner together that evening and dine-out in style.

"We're having a slap-up celebratory meal," announced my happy father and I will drive us to The Black Swan Hotel."

No whiskey then, Dad.

But earlier in the day I knew what I wanted to do; fairly certain that I would receive some birthday money from Aunts and Uncles and my one grandparent who lived a long way away, I would treat three of my very special friends to a fun lunch at the Wimpy Bar and let them order whatever they fancied.

And so it was arranged. Frankie and I caught the bus into town and there we met Joe first, and then Elsa.

I'd had a rather wonderful birthday present from Mum and Dad; it was a Kodak Camera which took Polaroid photographs. That meant it was instant processing (no waiting six or seven days for Boots to do the developing).

The four of us sat around a table chatting and laughing and having fun with the camera and eating burgers and chips washed down with coke or milkshakes and various ice creams for dessert. We were finishing our food and commenting on how full up we were when Frankie said, "Talking of food, I've got something for you Lizzy," and she reached down and handed me a hard flat packet. Clearly it was a book.

"Open it up then girl!"

I undid the wrapping and discovered it was a book entitled *Basic Cookery*. It was rather wonderfully illustrated and included everything from how to boil an egg to elaborate dinner party recipes. Frankie looked straight at me, "It's for the future," she stated simply.

Then to my surprise Joe, who has been carrying a rucksack when he arrived, bent down and rummaged and brought out another flat looking gift wrapped in plain blue paper. He gave me a funny look, "Something I made earlier, hope you like it."

I tore off the wrapping and we three girls crowded round to see. Joe had produced the most wonderful picture for me. Not exactly a painting, more like a pen and ink illustration and it was a type of cartoon depiction of our Wide Game. He'd drawn figures running around against the backdrop of woods and hills. In the centre was a two fingered signpost and on each of the fingers, pointing in opposite directions with an arrow, was the inscription: *To The Enemy*. It was beautiful, clever, ornate and perfectly executed and I was almost speechless and overcome with joy.

"Turn it over," said Joe gently.

And there, on the back, he had written *Easter Monday 1972: 'You can't catch me!'*

Elsa and Frankie weren't privy to the meaning but I was. I looked at Joe and blushed. Our eyes met and something told me that this picture would hang in a home for many years to come and Joe would have the greatest of pleasure in reminding me that, what I had announced in the heat of the moment on that delightful day in April, might not always be true as far as he was concerned.

Then, to my astonishment Elsa reached down and pulled out of her bag a gift with 'Happy Birthday' written on some very classy thick wrapping paper. I really wasn't expecting all these things and I certainly hadn't invited friends to lunch in the hope I might get something in return. Elsa went a little pink, "I hope you like it Lizzy."

It was flatter and bigger than the cookery book and a little more flimsy. I opened it and gasped with delight—it was the catalogue of the Temporary Exhibition from the War Museum. I could hardly believe it. I didn't even know there was a guide book, so caught up was I with looking at the exhibition I hadn't had time to go to the gift shop. I quickly flicked through the pages and there, of course, in the centre was a full page spread of Auntie Cath's photograph.

"Thank you, Elsa," I said. "You don't know how much this means to me." And she went a bit redder.

Just then a waitress came to clear our plates. She saw the camera on the table amongst the debris of the wrapping paper; "Here, let me take a picture of you all."

The four of us squashed up in a line together; Frankie, then Joe with his arm around me and Elsa to my left at the other end.

How different was this compared with the last time Joe and I sat in this very place? How much had happened since

215

then? And would I have ever dared to think that things could work out even better than my wildest imagination? Later when I got home, I would show the photograph of four very happy teenagers to my parents and I might tell them a little more about the one face they wouldn't recognise, but somehow I thought Mum might already be one step ahead of me.

So Frankie and I got the bus home and Joe and Elsa left together in the other direction—Joe to walk home and Elsa to get a lift from her dad who she said was coming to do some shopping. On the bus journey I looked at recipes with Frankie even though I was desperate to study the Catalogue.

We got off at the crossroads and parted; Frankie turned left and I carried on down the lane.

It was a beautiful sunny day mid-way through the afternoon and the hedgerows on either side of the road were full of the greens of early summer and the lush vegetation of grasses and wild flowers.

I was just sixteen and I had been out to lunch with three friends for a celebration, which, a few months ago, I could not have believed was possible. And now I was walking home—home to Dad, and home to Mum.

I was supremely happy, humming to myself and carrying my precious gifts carefully under my arm, thrilled with the wonderful presents I had received—each one so special in its own way.

But to my surprise there was a further parcel waiting on the doorstep; it was heavy and lumpy and wrapped in brown paper and tied with several odd bits of string and an old shoe lace.

A card on the top read:

To L M,

Spotted these in a French market and intended as a 'thank you' for Dog Duties. However, as we know other events took over the evening you brought Spoodles back and we all had our minds elsewhere. Trusting you may find them to be of use one day and I will be delighted to think you are safe!
Affectionately yours,
Catherine V-d-H

She wouldn't have known it was my birthday I was sure, but Mrs Van der Hayde had a knack of turning up at the right time. I opened the parcel and there lay a pair of beautifully painted, handmade wooden clogs.

Dad was next to me and picked up one of the shoes. He looked at it, puzzled. "What's the story behind this then, Lizzy?"

Well, Dad. That *would* be telling.

Epilogue

It was something to do with the weather that improved things (for her). *You can't control the weather, she thought, it's no use fighting against it.*

The sowing, the reaping, the cutting of the hay and the harvest were all weather dependent. Other jobs could be done when it was less clement—such as the laying of hedges—and some of the running repairs had to be done in any conditions if the safety of the animals was at stake.

Some tasks happened regardless of the weather; the twice daily milking, the feeding routine, the bedding down of the two Clydesdales at night.

And in the dark cold winter evenings certain engine parts or horses' harness found their way onto the kitchen table for it is kinder to the fingers to mend, clean and restore in front of a well-burning Rayburn.

But the times when there was no choice, when the sleet was coming sideways and the wind was howling round her hat, was when she felt most at ease—as if being at the mercy of the power of the elements meant she could accept her diminutive place on the earth.

Seasons change and the first year becomes the second and gradually the tensions ease. The passing of time, the restorative power of nature and the sense of rhythm and routine of the farming calendar; something happens to her and she stops resisting.

She knows she is lucky to be alive—to have lived—and gradually the war (her war) that is still raging in her mind starts to ease. Time heals if you let it. She spends more moments being grateful for what she sees around her and she learns to let go of the hatred, anger and deep sense of injustice. She smiles again at the silly things—the dog chasing flies, and she marvels at the miracle of new life—lambs and calves being born; chicks hatching from their eggs. Her spirits soar at the sight of the first swallows returning to nest in the barns for the summer.

Slowly, life as it should be felt is restored.

She will never forget of course—and neither should she. For when you have loved so intensely and lost so tragically you should remember those feelings and treasure the emotion.

And one day she knows, when the time is right and sufficient distance has elapsed, she will recount her story. She is not a hero, nor does she seek accolade, but she knows it is an important one to share.

She wants people to appreciate how desperate you might become to break the rules in order to save others.

And she wants you to understand that the only real way to enduring peace is to behave in a kind and reasonable way; to accept difference and celebrate diversity and never dictate how one should life one's life—what to believe in and how to express it. Personally, she believes in a Greater God which is beyond the restrictions of custom, creed and continent—for what can be good about any belief if it embarrasses or offends?

The Historian will do what is right. He will bring to life her brave and daring deeds of the past and interpret them to an audience that will come to see and hear and read and understand:

Give us wisdom that we might learn from the bitter memories of war.

And the young woman who sits on a stool in the kitchen with a dog at her feet and a clock ticking on the wall and a mug of coffee in her hands, also listens. She too, who has considered loss, hatred and forgiveness and discovered now what it feels like to fall in love, will one day tell a tale of some extraordinary moments when she was fifteen and a half. Her story will be set in the early 1970s; January to June. Only six months.

The two friends together sit.
And are silent.

Author's Note

The characters in *My Story* are fictitious as are the place names of Hillerton and the Bantock Hills.

You will no doubt find plenty of St. Stephen's Churches, and if you look hard enough some may have a Youth Club and their own hall (perhaps even called the Rectory Rooms), but the one in these pages does not exist under that name.

Biblical texts mentioned in Chapters 17 & 18 are from the King James Version of the Holy Bible, as are the words from the song, *Seek Ye First* (Matthew's Gospel Chapter 6, verse 33 and Chapter 7, verse 7).

There is no Chateau Hayde de la Dordogne but the main places named in France are real and the war story is as authentic as possible given the parameters of fiction.

Grateful thanks go to my friend Thierry Messaoui, for his assistance with the translation of French material.

Lizzy May Morrison is a pseudonym—she exists in my head. And now she does on paper.

Appendix

Promesse de Porte-fort

Je soussigné, Pierre Van der Hayde, déclare solennellement ce 10 juin 1941, qu'à ma mort, je lègue à mon épouse Marie Van der Hayde le château de Hayde et les biens mobiliers s'y afférant pour aussi longtemps qu'elle reste en vie (ad vitam aeternam), sauf volonté de sa part de s'en séparer prématurément.

Lors du décès de Marie Von der Hayde (ou plus tôt si telle est sa volonté), la totalité des biens sera officiellement évaluée et la somme en résultant sera divisée en trois parts égales au bénéfice des tiers dont les noms figurent ci-dessous.

En outre je nomme ma fille aînée, Louise Vormann, porte-fort pour l'exécution de ces clauses et dans le cas où celle-ci ne serait plus en vie, mon petit fils, Matthias Vormann.

Nonobstant la déclaration ci-dessus, un héritier est libre de racheter la part d'un autre héritier (avec son accord) si cela est dans l'intérêt de la propriété.

Fait à Saint Emilion, le 10 juin 1941.

Signature du Témoin : Georges Hubert

Nom du Témoin : GEORGE HUBERT

Profession du Témoin : VIGNERON

Adresse du Témoin : Rue du Forte Bayard, Saint Emilion

Nom des Bénéficiaires

ma fille : Louise Vormann
mon fils : Hendrick Van der Hayde
ma belle-fille : Catherine Van der Hayde

Pierre Van der Hayde